Alexander Wilmot

The history of the Society of Jesus

Alexander Wilmot

The history of the Society of Jesus

ISBN/EAN: 9783741191770

Manufactured in Europe, USA, Canada, Australia, Japa

Cover: Foto ©Andreas Hilbeck / pixelio.de

Manufactured and distributed by brebook publishing software
(www.brebook.com)

Alexander Wilmot

The history of the Society of Jesus

PREFACE.

As specimens of the Histories of the Jesuits published
in the English language, two taken up almost at ran-
dom are quite sufficient to show the ignorance, prejudice, and calumny with which the public mind in
Europe has been poisoned. One of these entitled "*A
History of the Jesuits, to which is prefixed a Reply to
Mr. Dallas' Defence of that Order—London : Baldwin,
Cradock & Jay, 1816*"—has almost the same effect upon
an educated reader of the present day as *A'Beckett's
Comic History of Rome*. But for the melancholy ignorance it displays, and the blasphemies it contains, this
book and many other books like it, could be ranked
among the most amusing literary efforts in the English
language. A few extracts out of hundreds which could
be given must suffice. At page 9, vol. i., we are told
that "The Jesuits have frequently excited the most
cruel civil wars in order to compel a whole people to
receive them against their will"; at page 51 it is stated
as a fact that "They (the Jesuits) established a society
of penitents at Bourges, whose object was to provoke

the anger of God ". The missions of South America
are treated in such a manner as to give this portion of
the work all the amusing qualities of a burlesque. We
are gravely informed that the Jesuits cruelly persecuted a Catholic Bishop ; but we can scarcely admire
his Lordship's prudence, as at page 99 the extraordinary fact is disclosed that " He was obliged to seek
safety among serpents from that implacable Society ".
But a Cardinal is made to do something even more
surprising, as in vol. ii., p. 324, we have it recorded that
one of those princes of the Church declared that " The
Jesuits do not believe in Christ," and a few pages
further on, at p. 325, we are told that "The Jesuit
Mourao called the Pope's Legate 'Lucifer'". It is
astonishing news to the Catholic world to be informed
(p. 330) that Pope Benedict XIV. " regarded the Jesuits
as a race of untractable and artful characters. He
issued more briefs, decrees, and bulls against them than
any one of his predecessors." But, according to this
author, anathemas against the Jesuits were of little use
as the " untractable " fathers were really the rulers of
the Vicars of Christ. He goes so far as to say that
" It is even a favour if such Popes as oppose the Jesuits
are not excommunicated ". But this bugbear order
was not only superior in power to the Vicars of Christ:
it even was above the moral law, as " The Society can
bind to herself others without being bound to them.
She always reserves the power of dealing with engage-

ments and contracts according to the interests of her own monarchy " (p. 354). At page 378 the greatest libel probably ever published is to be found. There we are gravely and deliberately told that " The Society of Jesus offers the bait of principles favourable to all the passions". The other English History of the Jesuits to which we desire to refer was published at Edinburgh in 1852, and purports to be written by " Nicolini,"* author of *The Life of Father Gavazzi*. This work presupposes an amount of ignorance and prejudice on the part of the Protestant public, for whom the book is written, of a character so gigantic as to be almost incredible. Of course Nicolini has been counting with his hosts—the Presbyterians of Scotland—whose general notions thirty years ago about Catholicism and the Jesuits could be made to furnish an exceedingly entertaining volume. Nicolini tells us in his preface that " English Jesuits do not regard Queen Victoria as their legitimate sovereign," and at page 299 that "The Jesuits alone have none but enemies among the other brotherhoods of the Church "; at page 293 we are informed that their conduct in " Protestant countries is a permanent conspiracy," and at page 164 some one is said to have been "persuaded by the Provincial of the Jesuits

* This History of Nicolini is to be found in several of our public libraries as *the* authority on Jesuit History. I have found it in the British Museum Library, where the History of Cretinan Joly is conspicuous by its absence.

that he could not perform a more meritorious action than that of killing his sovereign and benefactor". At page 146 the character of the saintly Pontiff, Pius V., is summed up in these words : " A more bigoted, fanatical, cruel, and sanguinary man never existed ". When a holy Pope is thus traduced we cannot wonder that the Fathers of the Society are said to proceed "stealthily as nocturnal robbers, mendacious in every word they uttered " (page 152). The great and noble missionary F. Parsons who freely offered his life for Jesus Christ is stated to have gone " from place to place to excite the worst passions of men's nature " (156). But it would be tedious to continue these extracts. In the preface the outrageous falsehood is told that " there is no serious and complete history of this wonderful Society,"* while almost in the same breath the author unblushingly says: " I have studiously not advanced a single fact for which I could not produce unquestionable authorities". These are specimens—perfectly fair specimens—of the books which are supposed to give Englishmen a fair and just idea of an order thoroughly identified with Christianity, and whose principles and glories are the principles and glories of the Catholic Church.

* The *third* edition of the great and complete *History of the Company of Jesus*, by Cretineau Joly, was published in Paris, in 1851, and in this work a long list of historians of the Society is given. There is no order which has more complete and reliable histories than " The Society of Jesus ".

If we wish to gain something like an accurate view
of the nobility and grandeur of one of the greatest
societies the world has ever seen, it is only necessary
to refer to the eloquent pages of a non-Catholic writer
whose genius raised him to a height so far above the
prejudices of education, that he could, as from a mountain top, see what to those of a lower elevation of
mind was completely hidden. Lord Macaulay tells
us, in the *Edinburgh Review*, that " All the pages of
European annals, during a great number of genera-
tions, testify to the power, policy, perfect discipline,
intrepid courage, abnegation, forgetfulness of ties most
dear to private individuals, profound devotion, infinite
prudence in the employment of means, which distinguishes the Jesuits in their warfare for the Church.
The Catholic spirit was concentrated in the breast of
the Order of Jesus, and its history is the history of the
great Catholic reaction. This Society has managed
the direction of all the institutions which most powerfully affect the human mind, the pulpit, the press, the
confessional, the academy. Where the Jesuit preached
the church was too small for the audience. The name
of a Jesuit on the title-page of a book assured its success. It was in the ear of the Jesuit that the most
powerful nobles and lords confided the secret history
of their lives. It was from the mouth of the Jesuit
that young men of the upper and middle classes
learned the first rudiments of studies reaching to

rhetoric and philosophy. Literature and science, so
long allies of incredulity and of heresy, were shown
to be allies of the orthodox faith. Become Queen of
the South of Europe, the victorious Society of Jesus
prepared itself for other conquests. In spite of oceans
and deserts, of hunger and pestilence, of spies and
penal laws, of prisons and torments, of gibbets and
quartering blocks, the Jesuits appeared under every
disguise in all countries—scholars, physicians, merchants, servants. They were seen at the hostile Court
of Sweden, in the old manor houses of Cheshire,
among the hovels of Connaught, arguing, instructing,
consoling, stealing away the hearts of youth, reani-
mating the courage of the timid, holding up the
crucifix before the eyes of the dying." The same
eloquent writer cannot but appreciate the evangelical
efforts of the order ; and, referring to its Foreign
Missions, cries out : " Noble enthusiasm, abnegation
rare and sublime, before which people can prostrate
themselves without fearing to incite numerous imita-
tors ! Enthusiasm, alas ! is in our time but a vain
phantom, against which is broken, equally, vainly, the
arid and cold eloquence of our preachers. But, in
truth, where are we to find it ? Will it be found in
the tithe markets haunted by our most sincere de-
votees, or under the sumptuous roofs of our opulent
incumbents ? Shall we find it in the hearts of our
regularly appointed missionaries ? . . . . Yes, we have

the faded enthusiasm of our makers of devotional experiences, the sentimental enthusiasm of our religious bazaars, the rhetorical enthusiasm of treatises where our charity perorates, the overflowing enthusiasm of our landed proprietor ascetics; but in what do all these enthusiasms resemble the intimate fervour, the divine emotion, the faith full of transports, of Francis Xavier?"

It is time that the masses in England opened their eyes to the truth, and saw the Society of Jesus not as a travesty—a hideous monster clothed in deformity— but as a great Order of Jesus Christ, preaching His name, suffering for His sake, and, as a good tree, producing good fruit. There should be an end to the silly, burlesque ideas concerning an order which has converted millions to Christianity, and produced such men as Ignatius Loyola, Francis Xavier, and Aloysius de Gonzaga.

The present work is merely an effort to present, in a popular form and at a popular price, a readable *résumé* of many historical facts connected |with the Society of Jesus. The great *Histoire de la Compagnie* by Cretineau Joly has not been translated into English, and is a work in six octavo volumes. The *Histoire* of J. S. M. Daurignac is a smaller book, but nevertheless comprises nearly one thousand pages. A good translation has appeared of the latter, but its price keeps it out of the hands of those very classes

most liable to be poisoned by the silly falsehoods
which have so long served to spread prejudices and
calumnies against the Catholic Church, by using
weapons of falsehood against one of its noblest
orders. Of course there are many other " Histories,"
but their size and price keep them out of the hands of
"the people". This small work only attempts to present
a rough and very imperfect outline of the progress of
the Society of Jesus, from its origin to the present
time. It is based chiefly on the large French *His-
toires* just quoted ; but valuable assistance has also
been obtained from other sources, among which
should be specially named the works of Ribadaneira,
Alban Butler, and Lingard, as well as the pages of
the *Dublin Review.*

PORT ELIZABETH, CAPE OF GOOD HOPE,
      March, 1884.

SOCIETY OF JESUS.

CHAPTER I

*Origin of the Society of Jesus.   St. Ignatius Loyola—his
character, life, and labours.   The establishment of the
Society.   The first Fathers, and their works.   Jesuits in
Ireland and in Italy.   Struggles against heresy. , St.
Francis Xavier and foreign missions.   His preaching,
miracles, and wonderful success.*

IN the sixteenth century two tides flowed strongly and
turbulently in the stream of history.   One can represent
the ever-enduring Catholic Church ; the other, the contrary
stream of heresy raised by human passions—strong but
evanescent, dangerous and troublesome—assuming to be the
real river, whose progress it could not stop but did its best
to impede.   God Almighty always raises up societies suitable for the various crises through which the world must
pass, and for the sixteenth century the Company of Jesus
was a moral necessity.   The nature, character, and work of
this noble order were all prefigured in its founder, Ignatius,
and, as a key to the meaning of the foundation, we must
carefully regard the life and works of the founder.

St. Ignatius was born in 1491, under the shadow of the
Pyrenean mountains, at the Castle of Loyola in Spain.   As
the son of noble parents he was brought up to be a soldier,
and distinguished himself both by valour and natural ability.

False ideas of worldly honour, vanity, and pleasure dis-
figured his mind, but he was impressed with loyal feelings
of religion, and used his undoubted talents in composing a
poem in honour of St. Peter.   The great soul of Ignatius
was displayed when the French besieged Pampeluna by his
retiring into the citadel with only one soldier when the gates
were opened to the enemy.   Acting under his encouragement, the best possible defence was made ; and when the
castle fell, Ignatius fell also, seriously wounded.   Like
another Saul, he fell only to gain a glorious moral resurrec-
tion.   When recovering from his wounds God Almighty
poured His graces into his soul through the channels of good
books, which were read by him for the purpose of relieving
the tedium of his illness.   His singular devotion to St. Peter
induced Ignatius to implore his intercession, and in the
silent watches of the night he was visited, in a dream, by the
great Apostle, who touched and cured him.   In the morning
he awoke well.   It was after this that the great change in
his mind occurred, as if St. Peter were determined to heal
his soul as well as his body.   Vicissitudes and fluctuations
of course preceded the great alteration, and it was then he
observed the ground of the rule for the discernment of the
Spirit of God and the world in the motions of the soul laid
down in the spiritual exercises.   Consolation, peace, and
tranquillity follow thoughts from God ; while those of the
world, although they seem to bring some sensible delight,
leave behind always some heaviness and bitterness.   The
triumph came at last, and God took entire possession of one
of those great souls capable of suffering, loving, and working in a degree rarely given to mortals.   In the dead of
night, filled with the utmost fervour, Ignatius is prostrate
before the Almighty, in presence of an image of the Blessed

Virgin Mary. He consecrates himself to the service of Jesus Christ under the patronage of His Mother. It is narrated that when he had ended his prayer the house shook, the windows of the chamber were broken, and a rent was made in the wall, which one of the writers of his life declared remained visible to his day. Before a great and arduous conflict great favours seem suitable. In a remarkable vision Ignatius beheld the Mother of God environed with light, holding the infant Redeemer in her arms; and so replenished did his soul become with spiritual delights that from this time forth for ever all sensual pleasures and worldly objects became perfectly insipid.

On entirely recovering from his wounds, Ignatius left his father's house and his rank in society. His first act was to make a general confession, which lasted three days, and then, staff in hand and scrip by his side, bareheaded, and in the livery of the poor of Jesus Christ, he set out on foot, directing all his thoughts, words, and actions to the greater glory of God. He fasted every day on bread and water, but made a slight exception on Sundays, when he ate a few boiled herbs sprinkled over with ashes. Each day he was present at the entire divine office, and spent seven hours on his knees at prayer. He attained to such humility that he went begging about the streets dressed so poorly and with an appearance of such wretchedness that children hooted and threw stones at him in the street. He had perfectly conquered himself, and was therefore prepared to conquer the world. His mortifications and austerities were continued on such a scale that at last he was found half dead and carried to the hospital at Manresa. Soon afterwards God Almighty was pleased to allow his servant to be tried by melancholy and scruples; but, having earnestly implored the divine assistance, he passed

out of this furnace of tribulation with a supernatural knowledge and sense of sublime divine mysteries which became
known to his confessors although carefully concealed from
the eyes of men.   Ignatius had become a Saint filled with
knowledge, and gifted with extraordinary powers of prayer.
As one of his greatest biographers says, he was raised to this
great position by humility, self-denial, contempt of the world,
severe interior trials, and assiduous meditation.   As the acorn
is to the oak, so was Ignatius Loyola to the Society of Jesus.
He contained in himself all that was necessary to form a great
order, and out of his bosom—out of his life—arose the
Institute which God designed him to establish.   He knew
what his work was, and became intent on carrying it out.
" It is not enough that I serve the Lord ; all hearts ought to
love Him, and all tongues ought to praise Him."   In these
fervent dispositions, and powerfully illumined by the Holy
Spirit of God, he wrote his Spiritual Exercises, which have
converted innumerable souls.   Here we have the most excellent maxims and instructions on the most intricate and
difficult matters, written by a man who was devoid of human
learning and could barely read and write.   He soon saw
that, in order to succeed in saving souls, learning was necessary, and applied himself to acquiring it with indefatigable
industry.   In the first instance he went from Venice to
Palestine, and, having visited the holy places, returned to
Europe in the midst of winter—January, 1524.   At Barcelona he humbly studied grammar, amidst the jeers and
taunts of the little boys who were his schoolfellows.   It is
narrated that the son of the person in whose house he resided
often observed Ignatius, at night, in his chamber, sometimes
prostrate on the ground in most earnest prayer, with his
countenance bathed in tears, repeating such words as these :

"O God, my love, and the delight of my soul, if men knew Thee they could never offend Thee! My God, how good art Thou to bear with such a sinner as I am."

It is impossible for any impartial person who studies the life of Ignatius Loyola not to sincerely love and admire this great and noble soul, who added to natural genius and native generosity the immense treasures of divine grace obtained by an absolute union with God. "I live, no not I, but Christ liveth in me," was exemplified. Humility, purity, unbounded charity shone forth in his words and actions. Everything he did was done for the greater glory of God. Severe studies were necessary, and he therefore devoted his powerful genius to the acquirement of learning. After studying two years at Barcelona he proceeded to the justly cele-brated University of Alcala, where he attended classes for logic, physics, and divinity. He lived in a small room at the Hospital, at which institution he held assemblies of devotion. For teaching the catechism "without learning or authority" he was put in prison. Without complaint he bore confinement for forty-two days, at the end of which time the Grand Vicar of the Bishop ordered him to be liberated, and by public sentence declared him innocent of any fault. He was hardly treated in his native country. At Salamanca he was again put in gaol, but the authorities felt obliged when he was liberated to declare that he was a man of sincere virtue. Ignatius from this place proceeded to Paris, where, after studying for three and a half years, he finished his course of philosophy and took the degree of Master of Arts with much applause. It was during this period that, having induced many of his fellow students to spend the Sundays and holidays in prayer and devote themselves to good works, his conduct was so maliciously mis-

represented as to induce the Principal of the College of St.
Barbara to order him to be publicly whipped. Ignatius,
considering that much scandal might result if this punishment were inflicted, went to the Principal in his chamber,
and so laid the case before him that this Doctor (Govea)
immediately took him by the hand and led him to the hall
of punishment, when he publicly declared that Ignatius was
a Saint, and had no other aim or desire than the salvation of
souls. In vacation time, during his studies, he had found
it necessary to go into Flanders, and once into England, to
procure charities from the Spanish merchants settled there.
Towards the end of his scholastic term an advanced scholar
of great virtue and ability was appointed to assist him. This
was Peter Faber, a Savoyard, born in the diocese of Geneva.

The spiritual exercises became a bond of union between
Ignatius Loyola and several men of great abilities and promise. The first of these was Peter Faber, the next was
Francis Xavier. The conquest of the latter was surrounded
with some difficulty, as his success in the schools had rendered
him somewhat vain. However, he was soon convinced that
all mortal glory is utter foolishness, and only that which is
eternal should be striven for. Three eminent Spanish
scholars followed. These were James Laynez of Almazan,
Alphonsus Salmeron, and Nicholas Alphonso, surnamed
Bobadilla. To these were added Simon Rodriguez, a Porto-
guese. These men, like the early Christians, had but one
mind. They made a vow to renounce the world and go to
the Holy Land to preach the gospel. If within a year after
they had finished their studies it would be found impossible
to go to Palestine, they were then to offer themselves to the
Vicar of Christ, to be employed in whatever service His
Holiness should appoint. It was on the Feast of the Assump-

tion of our Lady in the year 1534, and in the holy subterraneous chapel at Montmartre (Paris), that these vows
were made. It was on that festival, and under the auspices
of the Blessed Virgin Mary, that the Society of Jesus commenced to exist. Frequent conferences and exercises followed. Subsequently Ignatius found it necessary to visit
his native country; and so full of compunction was this great
and noble soul filled at the sight of the places where he had
led a worldly life, that he chastised his body with a rough
hair shirt, iron chains, and the discipline, besides passing an
extra portion of time in watching and prayer. In a public
discourse he declared that one of his reasons for returning
to Spain was in order to do justice to a poor man who had
been many years ago falsely accused. Ignatius when a boy
had joined in robbing an orchard, and this person had been
unjustly condemned to pay the damages. Two farms were
now given to him in reparation, and his pardon publicly
asked.

During the absence of Ignatius, the exertions of Faber
added three Doctors of Divinity to the Society. These were
Claudius Le Jay, a Savoyard ; John Codure, of Dauphiny ;
and Pasquier Brouet, a native of Picardy. Ignatius employed himself during an entire year in preparing himself to
offer the adorable sacrifice of the mass. At last, as their
mission to the Holy Land was rendered impossible by war,
the time came when it was necessary for the companions to
offer their services to the Pope. Ignatius, Faber, and
Laynez proceeded to Rome. It was at Vicenza that the
founder of the order declared that it should be styled the
Society of Jesus, because formed to fight against heresies
and vice under the standard of Christ; and it was on the
road to Rome, when praying in a little chapel between

Sienna and the eternal city, that our Saviour appeared to
Ignatius, shining in radiant light, but carrying a heavy cross,
and declared with infinite sweetness, " I will be favourable
to you at Rome".* Accordingly the companions were
graciously received in the holy city, and were able at once
to perform important work in reforming public morals.
Three Cardinals were appointed to report upon the new
order; and although at first they were opposed, their opinions
changed suddenly and remarkably, and His Holiness approved of " The Society of Jesus," by a Bull which bears
that title, dated 27th September, 1540. Ignatius entered
upon his duties as General on Easter Sunday in the year
1541.

During the sixteenth century, God Almighty was pleased
to open up immense fields for missionary enterprise by the
discovery of a new world in America, and the opening up in
the old world of the route by the Cape of Good Hope to
India. Soldiers of the Cross were wanted to resist heresy
at home and to conquer new worlds abroad. There was an
absolute necessity for a new missionary order, whose members would be men of great learning and ability as well as
devout Priests. They were wanted to resist the Luthers and
Calvins of Europe as well as the idolatry and paganism of
distant countries. The harvest indeed was plentiful, but
the labourers were few. When Govea, Principal of the
College of St. Barbara at Paris, recommended to the king of
Portugal that Jesuits should be sent as missionaries to India,
it was only possible out of the number of ten to send two ;

---

* This was disclosed by St. Ignatius to F. Laynez in a transport when he
came out of the chapel, and subsequently related by the latter to all the
Fathers at Rome, in a domestic conference at which F. Ribadeneira, one of
the biographers of St. Ignatius, was present.

but one of the men chosen was the great Apostle of the Indies, Francis Xavier. As the presence of Napoleon Buonaparte on the field of battle was always reckoned equal to ten thousand men, so in the field of missionary enterprise Xavier was for the battles of the Faith an enormous power. Nations became subjects of Jesus Christ through his influence, and the wonders of his eloquence, sanctity, and miracles are among the brightest jewels in that great crown of glory which encircles the Society of which he was a member. The additional vow of being completely subject to the orders of the Vicar of Christ at once increased the efficiency, and necessarily raised the status of the order, which became to the army of the Church what the household guards are to the army of a sovereign. For missionary enterprise such a vow was of immense importance, and greatly tended to the commencement and successful prosecution of foreign missions, as well as to the conversion of heretics in Europe. The great central power was now able to send first-class men immediately to any point, and this right we shall find was invariably used with wisdom and advantage. The Society soon became identified with the movements from Rome against unbelief in Europe and paganism abroad, and we cannot be surprised at the fact that it soon began to earn the deadly hatred and continued calumnies of the enemies of the Catholic Church.

Ignatius Loyola was a great legislator, and we find a proof of this fact in his constitutions or rules for the Society. The sanctification of the souls of each of his spiritual children by the union of a contemplative and active life is in the first instance laid down as absolutely necessary; then comes labouring for the salvation and perfection of our neighbour, by catechising the ignorant, instructing youth in

piety and learning—upon which the reformation of the
world really depends. The direction of consciences, missions, and the general work of an evangelist form the third
great division of work. No other habit than that generally
used by the clergy was to be worn. Choir was not to be
kept. Before any one was admitted to the order he was to
employ an entire month in spiritual exercises and making a
general confession. Then comes two years' novitiate, followed by simple vows of poverty, chastity, and obedience—
the order reserving to itself the right of dismissing the subject
at any time. Subsequently, usually after all studies had
been completed, second or solemn vows were made, binding
both sides, so that a professed Jesuit cannot be discharged
by the order from the obligations incurred by him to it.
On this occasion the fourth vow is taken of undertaking
any mission enjoined by the Pope. A class of Jesuits who
do not take this vow are styled spiritual coadjutors and temporal coadjutors. The great Suarez rightly calls the Society
the most rigorous of religious orders, in consequence of the
rule of Manifestation, which obliges every member to discover his interior inclinations to his Superior, and because
every Jesuit gives leave to every brother to inform the
Superior of every fault he knows without observing first the
law of private correction. These most perfect practices of
religious mortification enable men thoroughly to conquer
themselves, and thus be better fitted to conquer that world
which is the enemy of Jesus Christ and of His Church.
The Provincials and Rectors are nominated by the General;
but five Assistants, appointed by the general congregation,
have the various provinces so divided among them as to be
able to prepare and lay before the General exact information and definite advice concerning them. Each Provincial

must write once each month to the General, and is required every three years to transmit an account of all the members of the Society in his Province. Alban Butler truly says (*Lives of the Saints*, July 31) : " The perfect form of government which is established, the wisdom, the unction, the zeal, and the consummate knowledge of men, which appear throughout all these constitutions, will be a perpetual manifest monument of the Saint's admirable penetration, judgment, and piety ".

St. Ignatius frequently and strenuously endeavoured to resign the dignity of General, until the Pope forbade him to do so. So soon as he was appointed he went into the kitchen and served in a menial office under the orders of the cook. He continued to teach the catechism to poor children, while he preached with such wonderful unction and fervour as to bring back the time of the first Apostles, when multitudes were converted by hearing the Word of God. His heart so burned with divine charity that there seemed to be no end to his labours of love. A house for the reception of converted Jews, another of the Good Shepherd for fallen women, an orphanage, and an establishment for the maintenance of young women, whose poverty might expose them to sin, were among the first works of this great servant of God. Portugal, Spain, Italy, Germany, and the Low Countries began to ask for the assistance of the members of this Society. Francis Xavier was despatched to India, there to gain nations to Christ. John Nunez and Louis Gonsalez were sent to the North of Africa to comfort, teach, and assist Christian slaves among the Moors. In 1557 four other missionaries were sent to Congo on the torrid coast of Western Africa. In 1555 Abyssinia was supplied with thirteen Jesuit missionaries, one of whom, John Nunez, was appointed by Pope Julius III. to be Patriarch of Ethiopia. About the same time South America received the first of that devoted band who succeeded in converting nations and in bringing tens of thousands of souls to the knowledge of the truth. Our Lord was not only propitious to St. Ignatius at Rome: he most signally blessed his Society in Europe, Asia, Africa, and America. As a great mark of favour and of appreciation the Vicar of Christ appointed Father James Laynez and Alphonse Salmeron to assist as his Theologians at the Council of Trent. St. Ignatius earnestly counselled these learned men above all things to preserve modesty and humility, and to shun contentiousness and an empty display of learning.

Ireland was one of the first countries to which Jesuits were sent. That country, in which the greatest danger and the greatest affliction existed, was specially the land for the sons of Ignatius. Robert Archbishop of Armagh felt compelled to lay before the Holy Father an account of the cruel and inhuman persecutions suffered by Catholics in Ireland under the rule of Henry VIII. His Holiness, deeply affected, requested that two Fathers of the Society should be sent, and St. Ignatius lost no time in despatching them. These zealous men—FF. Salmeron and Brouet—traversed the entire island; but their presence was made a pretext for fresh persecution, and they were consequently compelled to retire. This period of the sixteenth century was most critical, as heresy attained alarming dimensions not only in the British Isles and Germany, but even in France and Italy. To drive back this invading tide was one of the special duties which devolved upon the Society, and to their success in doing so can be partly attributed the inveterate hatred which has animated all heresies towards them. The same Fathers who had been sent to Ireland were now commissioned to reclaim those who had fallen away from the faith in the towns of Foligno, Faenza, and Montepulcione. Their success was complete and remarkable. Father Laynez became a veritable Apostle to Venice. His magnificent eloquence caused crowds to wait all night around the church in which he preached, for the purpose of gaining admission early on the following day. The Lutherans themselves were drawn with the multitude, and were converted from their errors. A great miracle of grace was accomplished by this holy man in obtaining the consent of the Venetians to the entire abandonment of the pleasures of the Carnival. Exercises of penance and practices of piety took the place of frivolous amusements. The Doge of Venice presented the Priory of Padua to the Jesuits for the purpose of being used as a college, and in that city, as well as at Brescia, his services were of the most distinguished and important character.

The struggle against the Lutherans had become furious. The easy, accommodating, and agreeable doctrine about complete justification by faith, quite irrespective of good works, had deceived, and was deceiving, thousands. Jesuits conquered heresy wherever they appeared, and therefore applications poured in to the Holy Father for these valuable soldiers. The harvest was plentiful, but the labourers were so few that it became necessary to remove at once the original restriction which limited the number of the members of the order to sixty. Such a truly noble company could not fail to obtain recruits. Novices multiplied, and Ignatius himself watched over them, strengthening their virtue, and subjecting them to severe tests, so as to train up worthy warriors for the truth.

The first Jesuit college founded in France was at Billom, in the diocese of Clermont.   Among Catholic universities it is to be lamented that jealousy of the eloquence and learning of the members of the order, as well as that false spirit of independence which made them look with disfavour upon men who openly avowed entire submission to the Holy See, prevented the Jesuits from extending their influence as much as was desirable.   In Paris they had to bide their time. To the honour of Spain, however, it has to be said that these unworthy motives did not actuate the people of that country.   Houses were established at Burgos, Barcelona, and Valladolid.   The Viceroy of Catalonia (Duke of Gandia) declared that the Society was of heavenly origin, and promised to use all his influence for its propagation in Spain.

On the 7th of April, 1541, Francis Xavier sailed for India as Apostolic Nuncio for the entire East.   In all the lives of the Saints there is nothing more touching, beautiful, and pathetic than his entire career from the time he dwelt in the forecastle among the common sailors, during a long voyage, until the moment that, on the barren strand in the East which he had so much loved, he gave up his pure soul to God.   Immense ability and zeal, combined with intense love of God and his neighbour, rendered this great Apostle a Thaumatongus, whose conversions and miracles were on a scale in some way proportionate to his virtues.   No more capable or saintly man ever preached Christ to the heathen, and his work was blessed by his Master in a most wonderful manner.   Not thousands of individuals only, but absolutely nations, were converted by his labours; and if a proof were wanted of the sanctity, excellence, and admirable utility of the Society of Jesus, it could certainly be found in the biography of Francis Xavier. Let us merely glance in the briefest possible manner at his life and labours.

The Apostle of the Indies left Europe clothed with the ample powers and great dignity of Apostolic Nuncio. He was recommended by special letters to the monarchs of the East, and sailed from Portugal under the special protection of the king. Provisions of various sorts, although specially pressed upon him, were refused, and he positively declined at this time, or any other time, to have a servant. When Xavier was informed that it would be unbecoming for an Apostolic Legate to be seen cooking and washing his own clothes, he declared that he could give no scandal so long as he did no ill. F. Paul de Camarins, an Italian Jesuit, and Francis Mansilla accompanied the Saint. When F. Simon Rodriguez said farewell to Xavier, the latter answered an inquiry frequently before made as to the meaning of certain words which he had been heard to cry out in the Hospital at Rome. Xavier said that on this occasion, whether sleeping or waking he knew not, all the sufferings which he had to endure for our Lord were revealed to him, and that this revelation was accompanied with such delight that he therefore ejaculated, "Yet more, O Lord, yet more". He added: "I hope the Divine Goodness will grant me in India what He has foreshown to me in Italy". The mission commenced on board a vessel which contained nearly one thousand people. Xavier lay on the deck, lived with the sailors, catechised and instructed constantly. On Sundays, standing before the main-mast, he preached to all on board. With sweetness and tender love he checked gaming and swearing, reformed disorders, and, gaining the love of all, was instrumental in leading many from ignorance and indifference to truth and the practice of a good life. The sufferings and dangers of a voyage to India were at this period very considerable. Scurvy, pestilential fevers, want of good water, excessive heat, bad food, had all to be endured. After a voyage of five months Mozambique was reached, and at last, on the 6th of May, 1542, thirteen months after leaving Lisbon, Xavier landed at Goa. Vice, immorality, and neglect of the sacraments prevailed. There were not four preachers in the Indies, and no priest outside the walls of the seaport. After six months of untiring exertions a thorough reformation was effected. Youth was untiringly instructed in the practices of piety, sinners were converted from their crimes, and society completely regenerated. One plan of the Saint was to go through the town ringing a bell, imploring all masters, for the love of God, to send their children and slaves to catechism. With incredible labour, energy, zeal, and devotion, accompanied by miracles most fully authenticated, Xavier successfully brought thousands of souls to God in other portions of the Portuguese possessions. The process of the Saint's canonisation* proves that God at this time was pleased to restore life to four dead persons through the ministry of His servant. The first was a catechist who had been stung by a deadly snake, the second was a child who had been drowned in a pit, and the third and fourth were young people who had died of a pestilential fever. At this time the Saint used only to take three hours' sleep at night; his food was that of the poorest of the poor—rice and water. He was constantly teaching and doing the work of

---

* Nothing can be more searchingly severe than the treatment of evidence in the process of canonisation.   To deny that St. Francis Xavier performed wonderful miracles as an Apostle is to speak against the evident truth clearly established.

an Apostle. One of his biographers tells us that—"In the midst of the hurry of his external employments he ceased not to converse interiorly with God, who bestowed upon him such an excess of interior spiritual delights, that he was often obliged to desire the divine goodness to moderate them; as he testified in a letter to Saint Ignatius, and his brethren at Rome, though written in general terms and the third person. 'I am accustomed,' says he,* 'often to hear one labouring in this vineyard cry out to God: O my Lord, give me not so much joy and comfort in this life: or if, by an excess of mercy, Thou wilt heap it upon me, take me to Thyself and make me partaker of Thy glory. For he who has once in his interior feeling tasted Thy sweetness must necessarily find life too bitter so long as he is deprived of the sight of Thee.'"

St. Francis Xavier's success was as great as his sanctity, prudence, and capacity. Schools were founded, evangelical assistants, both Indian and European, recruited, and the permanent establishment of religion provided for. In the kingdom of Travancore he baptised ten thousand Indians with his own hand in one month, and it was not a very uncommon occurrence for the inhabitants of an entire village to receive the sacrament of regeneration in one day. It was at this period that God communicated to Xavier the gift of tongues. After this he never required an interpreter, but spoke in the various languages as necessity required. Sometimes five or six thousand people were addressed together in a spacious plain. He obtained the protection of the king of Travancore by causing a troop of robbers to retire from their work of plunder. Perhaps the greatest and most remarkable miracle performed by Francis Xavier was one

* Ep. 5, p. 80, Societate Romani.

specially required by circumstances, and specially calculated to impress people with the truth of the Catholic
faith. It was at Coulon, a village of Travancore, near
Cape Comorin, that he perceived few people were converted by his preaching. He then most earnestly prayed
that God would honour His beloved Son by softening the
most obdurate hearts. The grave of a man who had died
the day before was then opened by his orders, and he
called the bystanders to observe the noisome odours
which proceeded from the corpse. After a short prayer he
commanded, in the name of the living God, the dead man
to arise; and no sooner had he ceased speaking than the
dead man came out of his grave in perfect health. All present threw themselves at the Saint's feet and demanded
baptism. In the same country, on another occasion, he
raised from death to life a Christian whose corpse he met
when it was in course of being carried to the grave. To
preserve the memory of this wonderful event a large cross
was erected on the place where the miracle was performed. Our Saviour distinctly gave power to his Apostles
and their successors to prove the divinity of the Christian
religion by working miracles, and certainly no occasion
more required this extraordinary charitable interposition
of Divine Providence than when the gospel was being
preached to the heathen of the vast territories of the
Eastern world.

On the 25th of September, 1545, St. Francis Xavier
arrived at Malacca; thence he sailed to the Moluccas and
Spice Islands. From the Isle Del Moro, where he converted
the inhabitants, he writes:—"The dangers to which I am
exposed and pains I take for the interest of God alone are
the inexhaustible springs of spiritual joys. . . . I remember

not ever to have tasted such interior delights; and these consolations of the soul are so pure, so exquisite, and so constant that they take from me all sense of my corporal sufferings." In 1548 he visited Ceylon, when two kings in that island, as well as great multitudes of people, were converted. Having performed most wonderful apostolic works for all India, it pleased God to open up to him another great field in the isles of Japan, to which his attention was directed by a Japanese fugitive whom he converted to the Catholic religion. In 1549 he began to preach in these most distant and then almost unknown regions. He succeeded in obtaining leave from the king of Satsuma to preach to his subjects. He commenced by distributing copies of the Creed, and by means of miracles and preaching converted many people in such a thorough manner that they manfully withstood persecution for the faith. With incredible labour he proceeded on foot throughout the country, suffering like St. Paul the various hardships incidental to missionary work among strangers and enemies. In two several towns he narrowly escaped with his life, as the heathen took up stones to put him to death when they heard him speak against the gods of their nation. He returned to Court, only to be at once rejected because of his mean appearance, and then was compelled to don a rich suit and hire several servants. He took this opportunity of presenting a little striking clock and several other articles to the king. Three thousand persons were converted in this city, and two Jesuits were left by the Saint to confirm them and attend to their spiritual wants. The gift of tongues was frequently enjoyed by Xavier, and we find him at this time using it with great fruit for the conversion of Chinese traders, to whom he preached fluently

3

in their native language. It must be admitted that the admirable sanctity, meekness, and patience of this great servant of God often worked more powerfully than great miracles. Once when he was preaching one of the rabble, coughing up a quantity of phlegm, spat it full into the Saint's face, who at once furnished an heroic example of meekness by quietly wiping his face with a handkerchief and continuing his discourse. This created a wonderful effect. A learned doctor of the city then present declared that the preacher's virtue had convinced him, and shortly afterwards was baptised with great solemnity. Several others followed his example.

Having successfully laid wide and large foundations of the faith in Japan, and brought to God many thousands of its inhabitants, St. Francis returned to India in 1554, leaving missionaries behind. When at Malacca he determined to proceed to China. Like Alexander, he thirsted for additional nations to conquer; but this intrepid soldier had now nearly ended his great career, and it was God's will that he should receive his eternal reward at the threshold of that vast empire which was afterwards so successfully assailed by the Society. A small barren island, named Sancian, near Macao, on the coast of China, was the place near which our Saint gave up his soul to God. A fever seized upon him on the 20th of November, 1552; and on Friday, 2nd of December following, in a miserable cabin on the mainland, St. Francis cried out, "In thee, O Lord, I have hoped; I shall not be confounded for ever"; and the greatest and most successful missionary of modern times passed away to heaven.

An eminent biographer of the Saint tells us that "holy zeal may properly be said to have formed his character". In one of Francis Xavier's letters to Europe he says: "I have often thought to run over all the Universities, and to cry aloud to those who abound more in learning than in charity. Ah! how many souls are lost to heaven through your neglect. Many, without doubt, would be moved. . . . . Millions of idolaters might easily be converted if there were · more preachers who would sincerely mind the interests of Jesus Christ, and not their own." But the Saint required missionaries who are prudent, charitable, mild, perfectly disinterested, and of so great a purity of manners that no occasions of sin could weaken their constancy. "In vain," said he, "would you commit this important employ to any, howsoever learned and otherwise qualified, unless they are laborious, mortified, and patient; unless they are ready to suffer willingly, and with joy, hunger and thirst, and the severest persecutions." This Saint was a model of such preachers. In perfect resignation to the divine will, he preserved perpetual cheerfulness and tranquillity. He rejoiced so in afflictions and sufferings as to declare that one who had once experienced the sweetness of suffering for Christ would ever find it worse than death to live without a cross. He was fondly attached to the great Society of Jesus, and most faithfully responded to its spirit and instructions. Ignatius Loyola and Francis Xavier stand out in history prominently as exponents of the nature and character of that great order, which, like our Saviour Himself, has been the continual object of calumny and hatred.

Chapter II.

*Jesuits in Germany. The Society in Portugal. The Council
of Trent. South American missions. The Conference
of Ratisbon. St. Francis Borgia, Duke of Gandia.
Progress of the Society. Death of St. Ignatius. Calvinism. France. Calvin's opinion of the Society and that
of the Council of Trent. The plague at Lyons. Poland.
Foreign missions. The plague in Europe. Jealousy of
the Society in Portugal and France. South America.
The Calvinists murder seventy Jesuits on the high seas.
St. Francis Borgia and the battle of Lepanto. The
Jesuits in England and Ireland.*

I
T was in Germany that Protestantism first made the
greatest ravages, and it was to this country that Father
Lefevre was sent in 1540. It may be imagined that his
work was severe and his difficulties remarkably great from
the fact that in the city of Worms he only found one Priest—
the Dean of the Chapter—who was worthy of respect. He
at once was persuaded to co-operate heartily with the great
Jesuit, and the result was a complete reformation in morals,
and its sequence a return to the Catholic faith. At Spires
and Ratisbon Lefevre also reaped great harvests, and at
Nuremberg, just as great changes were commencing, he was
ordered to Spain. Fathers Claud Le Jay and Nicholas
Bobadilla took his place. The latter, when he preached

against clerical irregularities and errors of doctrine, was immediately assailed in the most virulent manner. The heretics, with loud cries of "Death to the Jesuit!" threatened to throw him into the Danube, but he replied, "What does it matter whether I go to heaven by land or water?" and continued his labours with great success.

Bobadilla so signalised himself by learning, devotion, and attention to duty, that each Bishop in Germany endeavoured to obtain him for his diocese. He remained, however, at Vienna, where he undertook the important task of reforming the priesthood, and the king was so pleased with his success in this most important mission that he appointed him his Theologian at the new Diet of 1543. There he refuted heresy, and proceded thence to the Diet of Ratisbon, where he met Father Le Jay. The latter, at Saltzburg, was consulted with respect and confidence by the assembled Bishops. Germany was an Augean stable, and the Jesuit Society became the Hercules of divine providence to clear it out. At Spires, Mayence, and Cologne immense good was effected, and, looking at the results, it seems miraculous that the tide of heresy and immorality should so soon have been turned by the few great and good men of the Society who were appointed to this duty. The heretics were so completely worsted in argument that they were obliged to use their usual weapon against the Jesuits—an appeal to prejudice and passion. The Fathers were chased from their homes, and were obliged to exercise their holy ministry by stealth.

Father Lefevre was now ordered to Portugal, and throughout that kingdom succeeded wonderfully in converting souls from vice. In the midst of his career he was commanded to attend the Council of Trent, at which Fathers Laynez

and Salmeron were also present.   He left immediately,
reached Rome at the beginning of July, and died in the
arms of St. Ignatius on 1st August, 1546.   So eminent
were the services of this great servant of God that it was
feared that he never could be replaced.   " He will be replaced," said the General; "a great personage will join the
Society, will contribute largely to its support and propagation, and, by his eminent virtues, will become an edification
to us all."   He spoke of the Duke of Gandia.

Each Father of the Society seemed a host in himself.
The unprecedented success which had attended their efforts
in Europe and Asia was to be repeated in South America.
Difficulties and dangers of the most appalling description
were overcome, and the great Church of God vindicated.
Si Deus pro nobis quis contra nos.   In 1549, Brazil was in-
vaded, and so generous and devoted were the efforts of the
Fathers who preached there, that the Governor, Don Pedro
de Correa, a member of one of the most noble families of
Portugal, entered the Society, and devoted all his labours
thenceforward to the "greater glory of God".   In 1553,
Brazil was constituted a Province, and Father Nobrega
placed at its head.   The wonderful growth and success of
South American missions will be referred to in due course.

Perhaps nothing more clearly indicates the position of the
Society, and the respect in which its devoted members were
held, than the fact that at the Session of the Council of
Trent, of December, 1545, two Jesuits appeared as Theologians of the Pope, and another acted in the same capacity
for the Cardinal Bishop of Augsburg.   These three Fathers
had received admirable instructions from St. Ignatius, so as
to prevent the great dignity to which they were raised im-
pairing their humility. They nursed the sick in the hospitals,

visited prisons, instructed youth, preached, and heard confessions. Nevertheless, their great and important duties at
the Council were in no way neglected. Father Laynez spoke
with such wonderful ability and knowledge that the rule
limiting speakers to time was specially made inapplicable to
him. It was this great defender of the Faith on whom
subsequently the Bishopric of Trieste was most persistently
pressed. He escaped with the utmost difficulty. Ignatius
earnestly prayed that God would avert from his beloved
company "the scourge of dignities," and obtained from the
Holy Father a promise that he would never compel a member of the Society of Jesus to accept an ecclesiastical dignity.

At the great conference at Ratisbon, where the Lutherans
were to prove that they were right, so as to induce peace
immediately by causing the Catholics "to leave the Church
of Rome in a body," Father Bobadilla triumphantly refuted
their arguments. Subsequently, when Charles V. published
his famous "Interim" decrees, the same Father pointed out
that the emperor had no right, upon his private authority
and personal responsibility, to tolerate the marriage of Priests
and communion under both forms. Bobadilla was ordered
to leave the Court, and the General himself was displeased
with his manner of acting. "If he were right in the
principle," said Ignatius, "he was wrong in the form. We
must never, even in the defence of the Faith and the
interests of the Church, be wanting in that respect which is
due to royalty and majesty."

In 1551, the Duke of Gandia, Viceroy of Catalonia,
became a Jesuit. The life and actions of St. Francis
Borgia shed immense lustre on the Society, and became an
additional proof of the holiness and usefulness of the
Institute of St. Ignatius. If any impartial person who reads

of the deeds of humility, abnegation, self-denial, pure love of
God and of his neighbours, exercised by this holy man, he must
come to the conclusion that the religion which animated
him, as well as the Society which guided him, were divine.

Of all countries in Europe, Germany was the one in
which the poison of heresy had most quickly spread, and,
to a great extent, this is to be accounted for by the
negligence and indifference of the secular clergy.   To
counteract this dreadful evil a college, which was to become
a nursery for Priests, was established.   Father Laynez, at
the Council of Trent, specially distinguished himself by his
wonderful erudition and labours.   Nothing could be more
convincing, definite, and clear, than his evidence from
Scripture and the Fathers in favour of the Catholic doctrine
of the Blessed Eucharist, as opposed to the new Lutheran
views.   But the humility of Laynez was even greater than
his learning and ability, for when being over persistent in
opposition to the General's views, the latter asked him to
reflect and say what penance he was disposed to undergo
for his fault ; his reply was that, after having consulted
God in prayer, he begged that he might be withdrawn from
his government of a Province, debarred from preaching and
study, and ordered to spend the remainder of his life in the
lowest possible employments of the order.   His penance
was to compose a compendium of theology, in which he was
to be assisted by two Inspectors of colleges.   Subsequently,
when peremptorily ordered by Pope Paul IV. to accept the
hat of a Cardinal, he fled for protection to the Father
General, and His Holiness yielded before this determined
humility.

At Saragossa, in Spain, the Society met with most extraordinary opposition, entirely based upon prejudice, and

which disappeared with its cause. In Germany, Catholicism advanced vigorously. In Abyssinia a check was received, as the king, whose mind had been poisoned, ordered the missionaries to leave. In Europe, the people of Corsica, who were almost in a semi-savage state, were once more civilized. In the Roman College there were one hundred pupils, the Pope had fully sanctioned the Society, the Spiritual Exercises had been approved. The Company had been only in existence sixteen years, nevertheless, it possessed a hundred houses or colleges, numbered more than a thousand members, and comprised twelve Provinces, including the Brazils. The work of St. Ignatius was done. At five a.m., on the 30th July, 1556, this great soldier of Jesus Christ was called from the Church militant on earth to the Church triumphant in heaven.

On the 19th June, 1558, Father Laynez, who had acted as Vicar General since the death of Ignatius, was elected General. Shortly afterwards the society was freed from its dependence on the Universities, and obtained power to confer on their students the degrees of Bachelor of Arts, Licentiate, Master of Arts and Doctor. At the period to which we are now referring Calvinism had infected a large portion of the south of France, and three fathers named Pelletier, Edmond Auger, and John Roger so well and successfully attacked its errors as to bring back the Catholics who had strayed from the fold. Strange to say prejudice and jealousy against this illustrious missionary order so prevailed in France, that for a long period the judicial approval of the letters patent, granted by the king to the Jesuits, was withheld. The reasons given for this extraordinary opposition were that the Jesuits "had excessive privileges accorded them to preach, and yet no particular practices by which they could be dis-

tinguished from the laity or common people, and that they
had not the approval of any council either general or provincial". This obstacle was removed by the Jesuits declaring
that they would only use their privileges in conformity to
the laws of the country and to the Church in France; and
they declared their willingness to renounce all others. The
Archbishop of Paris was satisfied, but nevertheless desired
that the Society should not use their distinctive title. This
could not of course be yielded. Facts like these give us an
idea of the difficulties and obstacles which the Jesuits had to
encounter even in Catholic countries. The objections to
their order were really based upon prejudice or jealousy.

The French National Council on religion, which was held
at Poissy, was attended by Father Laynez, who pointed out
the danger of holding these assemblies in accordance with
the wishes of enemies of the Faith. He gave great offence
to Catharine de Medici and to the Court but was forced to
do his duty. At this time Calvin wrote of the Jesuits:
"Use your best endeavours to rid the country of these zealous scoundrels who not only induce the people by their
speeches to rise against us, but blacken our characters,
impugn our motives, and represent our creed as visionary.
Such monsters should be dealt with as was done here in the
execution of Michael Servetus, the Spaniard." This unfortunate victim was burned to death for exercising that liberty
of conscience which Protestantism pretended to introduce.
F. Laynez proceeded from France to the Council of Trent
where his order was specially honoured in his person. This
venerable assembly specially recognised the services of the
Jesuits, and St. Charles Borromeo, writing to the Cardinals
assembled at Trent, said, "I deem it superfluous to adduce
the motives which move the Sovereign Pontiff to cherish the

Society, and to desire its admission into all the catholic provinces. As feelings of aversion are entertained in France against the Jesuits, the Sovereign Pontiff hopes that the Council, when it deals with the regular orders, will make honourable mention of the Society in order to recommend it."

On the 4th of December, 1563, the Council of Trent terminated its sittings. It had carefully investigated into the causes of the grave and wide spread evils which afflicted the Church, and found that the ignorance and immorality of a large number of the clergy and monks had to be remedied. Education was of course one of the principal means to this end, and the Jesuits stood in the foremost order of educators. Recognising this fact the majority of the Bishops requested that the seminaries and colleges of the order should everywhere be established. The Ambassador of Philip II. said that he only knew of two methods for ameliorating the condition of Germany and Spain;—these were to "train good preachers and to propagate the Society of Jesus".

In the History of Lyons by de Rubys we obtain details of the ravages committed by the plague, and of the wonderful heroism and devotion of Ff. Edmond Auger and Andre Amyot. The number of deaths exceeded six thousand, and public excitement and terror were almost unexampled. F. Auger earnestly begged the divine interposition, and the plague so suddenly stopped as to persuade the people that the prayer of this just man had been heard. The humble Jesuit was publicly presented with the keys of the town and entreated to accept the great educational establishment of Trinity College. On behalf of the order this new work was at once undertaken.

In Poland Father Canisius distinguished himself by a

brilliant victory over heresy at a great discussion held in the presence of King Sigismund. This good Father writing to F. Laynez says, "Blessed be the Lord who makes His servants illustrious by the hatred which the heretics excite against them in Poland, Bohemia, and Germany. By the atrocious calumnies they propagate against me they try to deprive me of a reputation which I do not pretend to possess. They pay the same honour to all the other Fathers. They are our persecutors, but they are also our brothers. We must love them for the love of Jesus Christ." The University of Dillengen was given into the hands of the Society. It was at this period that a very resolute and determined attempt was made to poison the mind of the Pope against the order, but the General at once and easily refuted the calumnies. "It is not surprising," said F. Laynez, "that the enemies of the Church should be also our enemies. They attack it incessantly and we are never weary of defending it. They seek to overthrow the authority of the Holy See; we employ all our zeal to uphold it. They endeavour to weaken and destroy the faith of Christian souls, and day and night we labour to reanimate and maintain it in all its purity." Pope Pius IV. not only became perfectly satisfied on rigid enquiry that the charges made against the Society were completely false, but that the order was in reality one of the most valuable in the Church. His Holiness showed in various acts his marked appreciation and approval of the Society, so that the calumnies urged against it served but to help on the work of God entrusted to its members.

Nothing could be more glorious or successful than the missionary labours of the Jesuits in foreign countries. India and Japan resounded with the name of Francis Xavier. The missions of Brazil, in South America, were most productive.

Unfortunately, however, in Africa the Society had to suffer, and, humanly speaking, to fail. In Abyssinia the Mahommedans obtained immense influence, and the so-called Emperors of that country absolutely prohibited Christianity. One of these rulers, named Adamar, became an inveterate enemy, and but for the intercession of his wife, the Empress, would have at once put the missionaries to death. A member of the Society sent by the Fathers of Goa was carried off and sold as a slave. Father Andrew Oviedo while straitened by persecution received intimation that he had been appointed Patriarch of Ethiopia. Without necessary food or clothing and subject to constant and most severe persecutions, he still made himself beloved by negroes and slaves, many of whom were brought to eternal salvation. His life however was a living martyrdom, and in order to reply to communications from the Pope he was obliged to tear out a few slips of blank paper still left in his breviary and to write, "Holy Father, I know not of any means of flight. The Mahommedans surround us on all sides. Not long ago they killed one of our number, Andrew Gualdamez. But whatever may be the tribulations which beset us, I have a great desire to remain on this ungrateful soil, so as to suffer and perhaps to die, for Jesus Christ."

In that great country which extends between the Limpopo and the Zambesi rivers in south-eastern Africa, ancient geographers placed the kingdom of Monomotapa. The Portuguese Port of Quillimane at the mouth of the Zambesi, was its principal gateway or entrance. One of the kings of the country named Gamba begged that Fathers of the Society might be sent to instruct his people. In response Fathers Gonsalvo Silveira, Andrew Fernandez and Acosta arrived in March, 1560, and were warmly welcomed by the king. In the kingdom then styled " Monomotapa," the king and queen with three hundred of the principal personages of the State embraced the Faith and were baptised. The Mahommedans here also became instrumental in stopping the progress of Christianity. They declared that the Fathers were magicians and at last succeeded in so poisoning the minds of many of the people as to induce a conspiracy against the life of the devoted missionary. F. Silveira was warned of this and calmly prepared to meet martyrdom with fortitude and faith. After having prayed during a portion of the night he calmly retired to rest. He was suddenly awakened by the fanatical Mahommedans, who under the command of a chief named Macruma placed a cord around the neck of their victim, strangled him, and afterwards threw the body of the martyr into the river Mosengessem.* Fifty converts were slain on the same day—the 16th March, 1561. The king, when it was too late, saw how he had been deceived and caused a number of the Mahommedans to be killed. Shortly afterwards Father Acosta died of fever and only one Missionary was left —Father Fernandez. A change took place at Court. Vice and sensuality conquered. The restraints of Christianity were thrown aside. The seed, which had grown up so quickly, had flourished on shallow soil where there was no depth, and consequently failure ensued. The remonstrances of F. Fernandez were in vain, and he felt compelled to cast off the dust of the place from his feet and depart to India. So far as the East African Coast Missions are concerned it

* A legend has been handed down to the present day about the body of the martyr having been protected by birds and wild beasts. See *Missions in Africa*, by Most Rev. Dr Ricards, Bishop of Eastern Districts, Cape Colony. In this little work interesting information is given about South African Missions which are now again being prosecuted in the Jesuit missions of the Zambesi under Father Weld.

may be mentioned here that they were prosecuted for some-time under the most serious difficulties. The climate of the coast is deadly to Europeans, and the miserable Portuguese Colonial Government could be expected rather to counteract than to co-operate in work for the real progress and civilisation of the country. Three hundred years passed away, and Livingstone, the traveller, found the remains of Christian churches. A healthy passage had been opened up from the Cape Colony in the south, and by this way principally did the last devoted band of Jesuits enter the interior of south-eastern Africa. This was the Zambesi mission. Several missionary martyrs fell, but their blood is but the pledge of future exertions, and again with renewed strength the Faith of Jesus Christ is being preached among the millions of natives in the regions of the Zambesi* who have never as yet heard His name.

On the west coast of Africa, at Angola, four of the Fathers were introduced to the Sultan by the Portuguese Ambassador. Unfortunately, here as in Abyssinia and in Kaffraria, Mahommedanism became inimical to the cause of Christ. The King was persuaded that the Jesuits were merely political tools of Portugal. Severe persecution was the result, and the Portuguese Ambassador advised their immediate departure. They would not go. "No," they said, "if the soldier, with the sole view of winning the favour of his superiors, does not hesitate in his obedience, still less can we Christians, priests, and religious, in our submission to God and to those whom He has placed over us. Our Superiors have assigned us this post, and here we will remain, at the peril of our lives, so long as we shall have not received orders to leave it." The result was that they

* Father Weld is now Provincial for the South African Missions.

endured terrible persecutions with patience and fortitude.
It will be never written nor ever generally known until the
day of general judgment what has been suffered under such
circumstances.

Africa seemed an unfortunate continent for the Society.
In 1560 a mission was sent to the Patriarch of Alexandria
with a view of uniting the Copts to the Catholic Church.
Fathers Elian and Rodriguez, when they arrived at Memphis,
were attacked and insulted in the public streets. A conspiracy evidently had been prepared, in which the Jews
joined. Public indignation was excited in the usual manner,
and the Jesuits became victims.

Father Laynez, the second General, died on the 19th of
January, 1565. The Society had only been in existence
twenty-four years, and it numbered one hundred and thirty
houses, and more than three thousand five hundred members.

On the day that Father Laynez was released from the
heavy duties of General, the great St. Francis Borgia, Duke
of Gandia, was appointed to this office. This great servant
of God was only fifty years of age, but the austerities of his
life seemed to have exhausted him. He was strong in mind
and heart, although physically weak, and so evidently wise
was the choice which had been made, that the Pope, on
hearing it, declared "The congregation could have done
nothing more useful for the good of the Church, more advantageous for your Institution, or more pleasing to the
Apostolic See ".

During the latter half of the sixteenth century the plague
at various times desolated Europe. In large cities frequent
panics occurred, when magistrates and men in authority
deserted their post, and the poor were left victims. In these
cases the Jesuits exhibited a heroism worthy of the Christian

religion. Magnanimous self-denial was shown in Rome, which called forth the special admiration and praise of the Pope. In Spain the Society obtained the love and respect of every good man for the noble manner in which they risked their own lives, and earnestly laboured during the fearful visitations of the plague in Cadiz, Toledo, Salamanca, Alcala, and Guadalaxara. This dreadful disease next attacked Portugal. In Lisbon the inhabitants became paralysed by fear. Numbers would have fallen victims of hunger or of the plague but for the unwearied labours of the Jesuits. The city was traversed by these devoted men at all hours of the day and night. Orphans and helpless children were carried to Asylums, the sick were nursed, and, above all, the sacraments were administered. The magistrates had fled, and the Jesuits were obliged to infuse courage into the hearts of the people, organise the administration, and inspire confidence. They succeeded in all this, and at the end had lost by death seven professed members, four coadjutors, and three scholastics. There is no page in the history of the order more glorious than that which records their heroic devotion in every city where the plague caused devastation and death. Ingratitude has been most painfully and most frequently exhibited to the Order of Jesus. The people of Portugal and Lisbon certainly well earned the stigma. After the Fathers had given their lives for them during the plague, they heaped abuse upon the order on a fictitious and absurd charge of desiring to rule Portugal. In all States of Europe, however, we find that profound jealousy has been at all times at work, particularly among clergy of loose morals, and among those indifferent pastors who felt inward reproaches at the contrast presented by the strict lives and hard labours of the Fathers of the Society. Among Pro-

4

testants and infidels, of course, the feeling against the order has always been that of profound and inveterate hatred. Vague, general charges alone, however, can be indulged in by them, and when these are probed to the bottom and thoroughly examined, it is found that they are utterly base-less and untrustworthy. In France, after a severe attack had been made upon the order by the University of Paris, which desired its expulsion from France, the venerable High Constable was perfectly convinced of the jealous motives for enmity that existed, and declared : " Reverend Fathers, I am not ignorant of all that your Society has had to suffer in France, especially since schism has publicly shown itself ; and you ought to bear those persecutions so much the more willingly, as they are similar to those to which the good are ever subjected ; and you know that all those who have laboured successfully in the Church of God have, like you, encountered innumerable obstacles ". Subsequently, im-mense services rendered to the French nation by the Jesuits caused all disabilities to be removed, and made them welcome in every Bishopric in the kingdom. Not only were they faithful priests and excellent teachers, but they were good loyal subjects, who were instrumental, by timely advice, in saving the country from revolutionary plots.*

So great was the good effected in Germany by the Jesuits that Father Canisius was styled the Apostle of that country. Poland was also revolutionised, and it was from this region that the angelic St. Stanislaus Kostka entered the Society, only to form a perfect model for Novices, and to pass, in a

---

* At Lyons the Calvinists had concerted to attack the city when the clock of St. Nizier struck midnight. Father Edmond Auger suggested that all the clocks should be put wrong. This was done, with the effect of entirely baffling and disconcerting the attacking force.

few years, to a better life on the feast of the Assumption in 1568. The principal enemies of Missionaries of the Faith were comprised in three divisions, including, respectively, heretics, infidels, and bad Catholics. Unfortunately, the servants of the Church were most seriously hindered by enemies who were nominally " of their own household ". Bad Catholics helped to originate heresies and to perpetuate them, while in India, and specially in South America, the bad rule and worse passions of men who called themselves Christians became most serious obstacles to the progress of the Gospel. The Spaniards in South America in too many cases disgraced themselves and their religion by a persecution of the natives, against which the Dominican monk, Las Cases, as well as numbers of the Jesuits and other missionaries, most earnestly and most persistently fought.

Fathers Martinez, Roger, and Francisco da Villa Real were despatched to Florida in 1566, and the first named of these was cruelly murdered by savages shortly after he had landed. Subsequently the Provincial, Father Segura, and also several assistants, were slain by the natives, who were enraged against all Europeans in consequence of the cruelties inflicted on them by the Spaniards. The blood of martyrs became in this instance the seed of Christianity, which quickly spread throughout the conquered provinces.

In Peru a lamentable state of matters existed, and Philip II. thought that to remedy the fearful evils under which this province groaned it was necessary to send Jesuits. This was done ; eight Fathers were despatched with Father Geronimo Portilla as Superior. The name of Xavier became a passport to the love and favour of the people, and the results were extraordinary. In one year the city of Lima was entirely reformed. Reinforcements were sent out, and the work of evangelising both the conquerors and the conquered was most successful.

We have now arrived at events which display in a very striking manner the extraordinary hatred of Calvinism to the Order of Jesus. Father Azevedo had reported strongly in favour of a large number of missionaries being sent to the new world, and was able at last to leave Europe with seventy coadjutors. They sailed from Oporto in a fleet under the command of Admiral Vasconcellos. F. Azevedo and forty missionaries were on board the San Diego, while Fathers Diaz, De Castro, and the others were divided between the admiral's ship and the galley which carried the orphans abandoned in the plague and now adopted and taken to homes in the new world by the Society. The "San Diego" became separated during a storm from the other vessels of the fleet, and, when near the island of Palma (Canaries), was chased by five pirates cruising under the command of a Calvinist named James Sourie. Our Lord had foretold that the persecutors and slayers of His followers should think they did Him a service. The crown of sorrow and of suffering has always been borne by the followers of St. Ignatius, and his order possesses the merit of not only having all things evil said against them unjustly for Christ's sake, but being perpetually in some country the special subject of outrage and persecution. The " San Diego " could not be successfully defended against an overwhelming force. Father Azevedo stood upon the deck holding aloft an image of the Blessed Virgin Mary. Twice was the enemy repulsed, but at last Sourie ordered his entire force to board. Leaping on the deck at the head of his men he loudly shouted, " At the Jesuits ! Death to the Jesuits ! No quarter for the dogs ! They are going to Brazil to propagate their false doctrines, and they must be exterminated." Constantly giving every spiritual succour possible to the dying men surrounding them, the unarmed missionaries were barbarously murdered. Father Azevedo cried out when being butchered, "Angels and men are witness that I die for the defence of the Holy, Roman Catholic and Apostolic Church". The grossest indignities and abuse were heaped upon the martyrs. In some instances, after having been maimed and cruelly beaten, they were thrown into the sea. In all cases, with one exception—that of Juan Sanchez, who acted as cook—they were inhumanly put to death. Thirty-nine martyrs had won their crown; and so impressed was a young man, who had determined to join the order, with the edifying deaths he had witnessed, that he stripped off one of the blood-stained cassocks, clothed himself in it, and, avowing his admiration for the order, was speedily put to death.* The ship of Admiral Vasconcellos was captured by the pirate Capdeville near the coast of Brazil. Thirty-one members of the Society were then massacred in consequence of the Calvinistic views of their captor. Thus out of seventy-one Fathers, novices, and brothers despatched to South America, no fewer than seventy were sacrificed to Calvinistic hatred.

In the Philippine Islands missionary efforts were vigorously prosecuted, and there, as well as in Japan, China, and South America, the "forlorn hope" of the Church made the first charge against paganism. Many fell in the assault : some by the hands of heretics, as in the case of the seventy sent to South America ; some by pestilential

* Benedict XIV. declared these forty Jesuits to be martyrs on the 21st September, 1742. Their names are all given in the work of M. Cretineau Joly, as well as in Daurignac's history of the Society.

disease ; some by the weapons of savages. Father Mascarenas, Superior of the Moluccas mission, had converted the
kingdom of Siakon in the island of Mindanas, as well as
Minado in Celebes, and Sanghir near the Philippines. At
length the hatred of the idolaters became so envenomed that
for eight days he was hunted like a wild beast, and at last,
when discovered in the forest recesses, was put to death on
the 7th January, 1570. Father Torrez, who was Provincial
in Japan for twenty-one years, and who died there when his
successor, F. Cabral, arrived, had been able to baptise with
his own hands more than thirty thousand idolaters and to
erect no fewer than fifty churches.

The last work of St. Francis Borgia, General of the Jesuits,
was one of the most important of his life. The Mahom-
medan power threatened Christianity and Europe in such a
manner as to make it absolutely necessary to form a powerful union in order to resist and overthrow it. With this
object in view Pope Pius V. requested the former Duke of
Gandia to use his best exertions as a negotiator. These
were eminently successful. The allied squadrons assembled
at Messina and proceeded against the Turks, under the
command of Andrew Doria. Three Jesuit Fathers accompanied the expedition, which, on the 7th of October, 1571,
gained that great victory in the gulf of Lepanto which
delivered Europe from the blighting scourge of a Mahom-
medan invasion.* St. Francis Borgia returned to Rome
from his successful negotiations, wearied and spent. This
holy General expired on the 1st of October, 1572, and was
shortly afterwards succeeded by Father Everard Mercurian.

* This victory had permanent consequences, as Mahommedanism was by
its means for ever turned back. The institution of the feast of our Lady
of Victories shows of what consequence it was.

In Belgium the Society had much to suffer from the calumnies of the heretics, who frequently excited the people to acts of violence, and in Germany a constant struggle prevailed ; but it was in England, during the reign of Elizabeth, that Jesuits won the most glorious crowns by patiently enduring, not merely calumny and outrage, but most cruel imprisonments, tortures, and death. Great Britain had become for soldiers of the cross a more dangerous country than either China or Japan, and its inhabitants more fanatical and cruel than the most ferocious savages of either Africa or America. The Jesuit colleges of the Continent, particularly that of Rheims, sent forth missionaries into this most dangerous field perfectly aware of the risks they encountered and of the fate that they would probably be called upon to endure. They were told very plainly of the dungeons of the Tower, of the rack, the thumbscrew, and the stake ; but volunteers were never wanting. Intrepidly they pressed forward, and there are no more glorious pages in the annals of any order than those which describe the lives, torments, and deaths of those apostolic men who suffered and died for Jesus Christ in England. The English Jesuit mission was founded in 1579 by order of the Holy See at the urgent request of Father William Allen, afterwards Cardinal Allen. Its first missionaries were Fathers Campian, Parsons, Sherwin, Kirby, and Rishton. In various disguises, rendered necessary by the penal laws, these men and their successors kept up the holy flame of religion in England. The very fact that they were compelled to assume disguises in order to do their work has been made a subject of reproach ; and nothing can be more false or scandalous than the statement that any of these men at any time conspired against the government. Imperative instructions to the contrary were issued, and were always constantly obeyed.

In the island of saints—Ireland—and in the Catholic city of Limerick, an incident of this period is highly significant. Father Donnell, a Jesuit, arrived in his own native country to preach the faith of an overwhelming majority of the people. He is apprehended and offered, not only life, but rich rewards, to apostatise. He refuses, and is immediately condemned to death and executed " for his obstinate impiety in professing Catholicity in spite of the prohibition of the queen ". While still living, his body was ripped up and his heart and bowels flung into the flames. A glorious death such as this served but to inspire the members of the order with special ardour for the missions in which the crown of martyrdom could be won. Every one knew that to preach the Gospel in England meant persecution and death ; still we find that the stream of missionaries never ceased to flow. While Jesuits were in course of being tortured in the Tower and executed on Tyburn Hill, others constantly pressed forward ; and from the time of the establishment of heresy, in the reign of Henry the Eighth, down to the period when the State Church poses as " Catholic," in the time of Victoria, the order has never ceased to supply the wants of the faithful in England. In times of the most severe persecution these Fathers were always found in the front rank, and the annals of the Jesuits in England supply testimony of the most glorious and the most edifying character. It is only possible to glance in the briefest manner at the numerous martyrdoms.* Father Campion was among the first seized. Neither he

* The very valuable annals of the Society of Jesus, published by Father Morris, supply details of the most ample and interesting character.

nor any other Father plotted against the authority of the
State, but simply for the crime of being a Jesuit priest he
was placed in a subterranean dungeon so small that he
could not stand upright.   After being detained in this painful prison, and deprived even of sufficient air for some time,
he was then cruelly tortured on the rack.   One description
of torture freely indulged in was that of stating falsely to
Jesuit Fathers that their colleagues had betrayed not only
family secrets, but those of the confessional.   Father Campion, when informed by a brother martyr of the affliction
which one of these reports had caused him, said : " I feel
that I have the courage, and I trust that God will give me
the strength, never to allow them to force from me, by all the
tortures they may apply, a single word that may be prejudicial to the Church of Jesus Christ".

CHAPTER III.

Sufferings of Jesuits in England. The Gunpowder Plot. Persecutions in Scotland and Ireland. Missions in South America. Missions in North America.

FATHER Campion, an English Jesuit Martyr, chanted the *Te Deum* when his flesh was being torn and his limbs dislocated under torture. At last, by a glorious death on the scaffold, he sealed his confession. The charge of high treason brought against this priest and other Jesuits was utterly false and malicious. It was most certainly neither the wish nor the interest of the order to meddle with politics in England,* and their Fathers received the strictest instructions in no case to do so. As missionaries it was perfectly clear their efforts would be partially neutralised if they took any part against the existing Government of the country. Nevertheless, from Babington's plot in the reign of Elizabeth to the great papist plot of Titus Oates in the time of James the Second, we find the same foul and malicious falsehood constantly warring against them. They are always charged with high treason, but the offence was never once proved; on the contrary, nothing is more evident than their innocence; yet, so great is the effect of

---

* See this clearly proved in Lingard, and in the Annals of the order, by F. Morris.

prejudice, that even to the present hour in England justice cannot be obtained for the memory of those great and holy confessors of Christ. The mere mention of a few cases of martyrdom indicates what manner of men they were. Father Thomas Cottam was hanged and disembowelled when still alive, after having undergone the torture of the Scavenger's daughter, which is thus described :—" It consisted of two semicircles of iron joined together at one end, the other end was turned in a contrary direction, and by means of a link the two formed a hoop which could be contracted at pleasure. The victim was placed on his knees on the point where the two semicircles were joined ; the executioner pressed down the head and chest, and applied all the force of his body upon the unfortunate sufferer, until he was able to join together the two semicircles by the ends that were turned outward. The victim was thus transformed into a sort of ball, in which the human being could be discovered only by the blood which gushed from his nostrils, hands, and feet." Jesuits were hunted down as if they were the most infamous of mankind.. They were condemned without reason and without proof. The principle that the end justifies the means which has invariably been condemned by the order and by the Church was unscrupulously adopted against them. Camden, the Protestant historian, tells us in his Annals that Elizabeth's government "had recourse to fraud to discover the secrets of hearts. Letters were fabricated purporting to come clandestinely from the Queen of Scotland and the banished Catholics. These were introduced into the houses of the Papists in order that they might there be found and used against them. Numerous spies were to be found in every direction for the purpose of reporting whatever might be said or done, and no matter who was the informer, or how unimportant the intelligence, he was admitted as a witness." The doctrine of the means justifying the end was in reality not used by the Jesuits, but against them.

The terrible persecution of Catholics in England maddened several Catholic noblemen and gentlemen. For merely professing the religion of their forefathers they were systematically robbed under the authority of penal laws which inflicted heavy fines. For being a Catholic, property and life were forfeited. An infamous system of informing was in force, and the utter destruction of Catholicism was threatened. These desperate men were few in number, and the Jesuits in no way participated in their wild and foolish conspiracy. In fact the absurd plot for blowing up the Parliament with gunpowder was known to the ministry of James the First who made political capital out of it. Nothing could more have played into the hands of the persecutors, and nothing could be more opposite to the instructions, wishes, and views of the Jesuits. In fact, the madmen who intended to commit wholesale murder contemplated a crime opposed to the first principles of Christianity, and were merely tools of Cecil and the British Government.* Father Garnet, the Provincial, writing on the 8th of May, 1605, to Father Parsons, says :—" Divers Catholics are offended with Jesuits. They say that Jesuits do impugn and hinder all forcible enterprises. I dare not inform myself of their affairs, because of prohibition of Father-General for meddling in such affairs." This Provincial (Garnet) had entreated the Holy See to threaten with excommunication all those who should become asso-

* See, *inter alia*, for clear evidence of this, Lingard and the Annals of the Jesuits, by Morris.

ciated in any conspiracy. Seditious plots were most contrary to the interest and duty of Catholics. In a letter to the General, the English Provincial is compelled to state: "All the English Catholics are not obedient to the Pope's commands. . . . They openly say that they will take good care not to make known their intentions to the priests. They complain more especially of us, because we oppose their machinations."

Catesby, one of the principal conspirators, fearing that the Jesuits might communicate their suspicions to the Government, adopted the bold and wicked course of disclosing the entire plot to Father Greenway (Father Oswald Texmund), under the sacred seal of confession. The confessor endeavoured in vain to divert him from the awful project. The conspirators were fanatics, and no eloquence, zeal, nor authority had any effect upon them. Catesby would only make one concession, and that was to give authority for Father Greenway to confer with the Provincial under that seal of confessional secrecy which he knew could not, under any circumstances, be broken. Francis Tresham, one of the conspirators, gave information to the Government, and the Ministers of Elizabeth were most certainly well aware of the plot sometime before the day fixed for its execution. On the 5th of November a theatrical denouement took place, when the barrels of gunpowder were discovered under the Houses of Parliament. Guy Fawkes suffered the most frightful tortures without revealing the names of his accomplices, until he heard they had taken up arms. Then he considered that concealment was unnecessary. The conspirators were only seven or eight in number, and their efforts found no response among the many thousands of Catholics in the Kingdom. The Jesuits had most

thoroughly opposed all such attempts against the established
Government, and the only Father of the Society who knew
of the plot was unable, under the seal of confession, to
speak of it; but, nevertheless, did his utmost to frustrate
and prevent it.   Catholicism detested and anathematised
all such undertakings, and distinctly pointed out that they
were contrary to the law of God.   Besides, such a rash
scheme as the gunpowder plot was so clearly foolish and
contrary to the interests of Catholics, that no man of common sense or prudence could, in any point of view, favour
it.   The truth is, it was well calculated to play into the
hands of the fanatical and malignant enemies of the Church,
and was concerted, or at least fomented and encouraged in
their interests.*   Every possible advantage was immediately
taken of it.   The hell-dogs of persecution and malignant
bigotry were immediately loosed.   The Protestant ministers
persistently declared that "the plot" was the fruit of a
Catholic conspiracy, which owed its origin to the Pope and
to the King of Spain.   The Jesuits were, of course, the
principal instruments, and they should be exterminated like
wild beasts.   The furious hatred of the populace was stirred
up against them, and the order was held up to universal
execration.   There was a thorough exemplification of our
Saviour's words : "They have hated me without cause".

Fathers Garnet, Texmund (Greenway), and Gerard were
arrested.   They were condemned before trial, as the edict
for their apprehension states that "it is evident and positive
that all three have been direct abettors of the conspiracy,
and, in consequence, are not less guilty than the actual

---

* There is very good evidence to prove that the plot was, at the commencement, known to the Government, and that they fomented and encouraged it.

perpetrators and concoctors of the plot ". The depositions
of the prisoners were shamelessly interpolated with statements against the Jesuits. So much so that Fawkes, indig-
nantly pointing out that this infamous course had been
adopted, exclaimed : " Why is the attempt made to interpo-
late in our evidence that which is so opposed to the truth ".
On the scaffold, when about to be executed, Fawkes and
the other real conspirators emphatically declared aloud the
perfect innocence of the Jesuits.

Fathers Oldcorne and Garnet were placed together in the
same room at the Tower, and there, thinking they were
alone, the latter said : " There exists no evidence that they
made me acquainted with it (the plot); there is but one
living being can say so ". This was heard by an appointed
spy, and construed into a confession of guilt, although it
merely alluded to the fact that in the Sacrament of Confession, whose seal is perfectly inviolable, a disclosure of the
plot had been made. Father Garnet had now to submit to
the most frightful tortures, and at last, on the 3rd of May,
1606, the Provincial died gloriously on the scaffold. The
next martyr unjustly condemned was Father Oldcorne, who
was executed on the 17th of April, absolutely for the crime
of neither ." approving nor condemning the plot, therefore
for having approved of it ". On the 23rd of June Father
Thomas Garnet, nephew of the Provincial, was put to death
simply for being a Jesuit. His life was offered to him if
he subscribed a certain oath, and the Earl of Exeter
added : "You may even use mental reservation ". " Life and
liberty are of little importance to me," replied the Father,
and he chose death before dishonour.

While these events were taking place in England the
enemies of the Catholic Church in Scotland considered it a

great triumph to bring to the scaffold a Scottish Jesuit—
Father Ogilvie. His crime was saying Mass and performing
the duties of his office in Glasgow. Presbyterianism always
displayed the most malignant hatred for that creation of
their imagination "Popery," and in killing priests or bishops
thought "that they were doing God a service". Father
Ogilvie was executed as if he were a common malefactor,
and died steadfastly professing his faith. So long as penal
laws and persecution existed in the British Isles, so long
were the Jesuits in the front as a "forlorn hope" sent out
against the citadel of heresy. Their dangers and sufferings,
as well as their services, were always greatest. The hatred
against them, entirely based upon calumnies, was perfectly
unexampled. It is impossible even to furnish a bare catalogue of martyrs. Speaking of the era of Elizabeth, we are
told by Cretineau Joly in his History of the Society (Vol.
II., p. 252), that it is impossible to recount each of the
cases of torturing and death which the Jesuits suffered.
Under the rule of Elizabeth, Fathers Cornelius, Walpole,
Bosgrave, Filcock, Southwell (the poet), Page, and a hundred others perished under the newly invented punishments
which were so horridly cruel that, in the opinion of Condorcet,
they would have terrified the imagination of a savage. In
James the First's time "the plot" helped Protestantism to
glut its rage against the Society, and when Charles came to
the throne the Puritans, whose ascendency caused the destruction of that monarch, "showed themselves insatiable of
blood and of liberty". A Father, Edmond Arrowsmith,
completely conquered an Anglican bishop in a great theo-
logical dispute, but the executioner supplied the defects of
Protestant reasoning, and on 7th of September, 1628, in
the same year of the religious dispute, the Jesuit perished

upon the scaffold. Puritan bigotry and intolerance were always very intense. In illustration of this, we find that in the month of June, 1642, Parliament presented the draft of a treaty to Charles the First, one of whose articles provided that "The edicts in force against Jesuits, priests, and recusant papists shall be rigorously executed, without any tolerance or dispensation". When, shortly afterwards, Father Thomas Holland was brought before a jury, it was quite sufficient to charge him with being a Jesuit. This was enough. To kill him was to do God a service, and he was accordingly iniquitously found guilty, and iniquitously executed. There was no juridical proof even that he was a Jesuit, still less was there a shred of evidence connecting him with plots against the Government of the country. Father Rodolph Corby, an Irish Jesuit, when brought before a jury, declared that he was a member of the Society, and for that heinous crime was hanged, and, when still alive, disembowelled. On the night before he died the French Ambassador, the Duchesse de Guise, and other members of nobility heard mass in his cell, and subsequently accompanied him on his way to the scaffold. Fathers Bradley, John Grose, Cuthbert Prescott, and Edmund Nevil died under the infliction of cruel imprisonment and torture.

Under Oliver Cromwell, Father William Bayton of Cashel fell by the sword, while Fathers Robert Netervil, Henry Carel, and John Bath succumbed to the cruelties of the "lovers of the gospel". The Republic, which hypocritically declared that it established liberty, most rancorously persecuted Catholics for simply professing their religion, and Jesuits were, of course, proscribed and banished. The members of the Society in Ireland gloriously remained in the midst of persecution, to cement with their blood the

5

union of steadfast faithfulness, which bound the people to the faith of their fathers. The most determined effort was made to make the "island of faith" Protestant. Numbers of Catholics were banished or driven forth of the country, and anabaptists, &c., planted on the soil. All, however, was in vain, and it is to the everlasting glory of the Society of Jesus that its devoted members would not desert Ireland in this time of great danger and most severe trial, but materially assisted in keeping the people true to the Catholic faith.

We must now advert to the great Jesuit missions of South America. As has been already mentioned, seventy-one missionaries for Brazil were massacred by the Calvinists in 1572, but this apparent loss seems to have been in reality a great gain to the Society, as from that period most wonderful success crowned the efforts of the Fathers in the new world, so that tens of thousands of souls were brought to Christ. Father Toledo landed on the Brazilian coast in 1573, with 12 companions. Among the barbarous tribes miracles of conversion were effected. The missionary proceeded in most apostolic guise, barefooted, with his rosary round his neck, and his crucifix at his side, carrying on his back a small altar and some vestments. In the gentlest manner, and with the utmost affection, the pagans were addressed and won over. At first, great suffering and great losses had to be endured. Father Antony Lopez was poisoned in Peru by savages in 1590, and Father Miguel Urrea was slain by the natives a few days afterwards. In 1604 there were fifty-six Jesuits in this dangerous field. Soon it was necessary to erect Peru into three vice-provinces, namely Chili, Tucuman, and Paraguay. When a serious revolt took place among the Araucanians in Chili, the Jesuits promised the malcontents that the King of Spain would

pardon those who would accept the religion of Jesus Christ
and make themselves worthy of baptism. Revolt and blood-
shed ceased, and real conversions soon became numerous.
Father Valdivia left for Spain, and then, at his special
request, the independence of this people was fully conceded.
On his return the Araucanians overwhelmed him with testimonies of gratitude. Everywhere the Jesuits were the
enemies of slavery, and it was through their untiring efforts
that numbers of tribes were emancipated from bondage. In
testimony of esteem for Father Joseph Anchieta, whose
wonderful zeal and charity for slaves had secured general
admiration, the Spanish Government forbade the enslave-
ment of any Brazilians.

In 1615 the Society numbered no fewer than sixty-two
members at Rio de Janeiro and Pernambuco, forty in the
neighbouring towns, and fifty-six at Bahia. Two opposing
forces warred in the new world, one in favour of the
natives, the other against them. Avaricious and unprin-
cipled Europeans desired to continue slavery, and to rob the
aboriginal inhabitants not only of their property but even of
their civil rights. Cruel injustice in many cases prevailed,
and in this way serious obstacles were raised to the progress
of Christianity. The missionaries of the Catholic Church
fought with the utmost zeal and courage for the oppressed.
We find men like the great Dominican, Las Casas, performing prodigies, and the members of the Society of Jesus
were always gloriously in the front rank of the friends of the
natives. At Carthagena in New Granada, Father de Sand-
oval spent his life in instructing the negroes continuously
arriving at that great mart of slaves. Father Peter Claver
was beatified by the Church. He styled himself, and was
in reality "the slave of slaves". To learn the wonderful success

of charity blessed by God, we have only to look at the miraculous progress of the Society in converting the Guaitos of Brazil. This was a ferocious tribe of cannibals whom the Fathers attacked, armed with crucifix and confidence in God. Mildness and kindness exercised the most wonderful effects—the first converts were appointed catechists, and soon the tribe became Christian. The greatest successes were obtained in erecting peaceful happy communities throughout the length and breadth of Paraguay. Marvels of Christian civilisation were performed, which have elicited the esteem and admiration of Protestants and unbelievers. The Presbyterian writer, Robertson, tells us in his *History of Charles the Fifth* (Vol. II., p. 229) : "It is in the new world that the Jesuits have exercised their talents with the greatest eclat, and in the manner most useful for the human race ". The naturalist, Buffon, says (Tome **XX.**, *de l'Homme*, p. 282) : "Sweetness, charity, good example, the exercise of virtue constantly practised among the Jesuits have touched the savages and conquered their defiance and their ferocity ; they have themselves asked to be made acquainted with the law which renders men so perfect. Nothing has more honoured religion than having civilised those nations, and laid the foundations of an empire without any other arms than those of virtue." The celebrated Haller says : (*Traite sur divers sujets*, p. 120) : "The enemies of the Society depreciate its best institutions. They accuse it of unmeasured ambition when they see a species of Empire formed in a distant country, but what project can be more beautiful and advantageous to humanity than that of collecting people dispersed amidst the wilds of America, and of drawing them from their savage state, which is one of misfortune ; to stop their cruel and distructive wars ; to enlighten them with the rays of the true religion ; to unite them into one society which represents the golden age by the equality of its citizens and the community of its goods. An ambition which produces so many advantages is ‘ a laudable passion ’.” Cretineau Joly truly and eloquently adds (Tome III., p. 228) : “ The Jesuits, in fact, were able to realise the Utopia of which philosophers had dreamed, and which all serious men had regarded as impossible. From St. Francis Xavier to Father de Brebœuf; in Japan and Ethiopia, in India and in Peru, in Brazil and in Mongolia, in most arid plains, and in Monomotapa, in the depths of forests as on the banks of the Bosphorus, under the cedars of Lebanon as in the huts of savages, in China and in Canada, in the Indies and in Thibet, we have seen them, according to the advice of the apostle, gentle with the suffering, little with the weak, mild with barbarous natures, learned with cultivated minds, diplomatists with the powers of the earth, at each hour ready to devote life to convert a soul, or to announce the truth to mankind. They are literary men and mandarins in China, slaves of negroes at Carthagena, Brahmahs and Pariahs in Hindostan, wandering hunters in Canada, Maronites under the palms of Judea. They follow St. Paul, and become all things to all men that they may gain souls to Christ. ”

In Paraguay the Society was at first untrammelled, but soon found itself between two great dangers. These were the avarice and rapacity of the Spanish colonists and the savage character of the natives. Most successfully did they navigate between this Scylla and Charybdis, but they had to exercise the most wonderful fortitude and patience. By gentleness, kindness, and the arms of Christian charity, under the blessing of God, the aboriginal inhabitants were converted, while able and well-sustained appeals to the King

of Spain secured his powerful intervention. The jealous
hatred of the Spaniards, who saw the natives taken out of
their grasp, presented very serious and very galling obstacles.
The great conquerors from Europe looked upon the poor
aborigines as their natural thralls and bondsmen. They refused alms to the missionaries, and frequently the Jesuits
had to subsist on herbs, roots, and Indian corn. They
were resolved that death alone should separate them from
their flock. The name " Loretto " was given to the first
" Reduction " or settlement, and the Indians hastened there,
and were allowed to erect dwellings. Each trade had its
workshop. Carpenters, locksmiths, carvers, painters, weavers,
builders, were instructed, and each person was allowed to pursue that occupation which was most congenial to him. Agri-
culture found few admirers, and the fathers had themselves
frequently to guide the plough. Reduction followed Reduction. Little towns sprung up, in which there were
churches, well-built houses, regular streets, and all the com-
forts of civilisation. Each town was governed by two of the
Fathers, one of whom was pastor and the other vicar. Each
citizen owned a portion of ground, and every year a part of
the harvest was stored away as a resource against disaster.
Under the kind paternal rule of the Society, peace, tranquillity, success, and happiness were secured. No negotiations with the Spaniards were permitted except through the
intermediary of the Fathers. Several other tribes entered
Paraguay, and were incorporated in its republic, which became unparalleled in the history of the world as a proof of
the happiness which could be made to result from the unity
of industry and religion under a government animated by
Christian charity. The Bishop of Buenos-Ayres reported
that he was amazed at the incredible success of the Jesuits,

and said that he "did not think in a whole year a single mortal sin was committed in these reductions ". One of the serious dangers which threatened the mission arose from the enmity of savage tribes on the Brazilian frontiers, who ravaged and destroyed the beautiful Reductions of St. Joseph, St. Francis Xavier, St. Peter, Conception, St. Ignatius, and Loretto. The Spaniards would render no assistance, and ironically called upon the Fathers, as they had sought to govern the Indian Natives, now to defend them. This they did most efficaciously. Their enemies were repulsed, while many of those who were captured became good Christians. So great was the success attendant on the Paraguay Mission that, in 1656, the Jesuits had converted and civilised more than one hundred and fifty thousand savages. They had done much more, as they had established great civilised communities where there was real brotherly unity with the simplicity and purity of primitive Christianity. From this great success the Fathers in South America turned their attention to a greater—no less than the conversion and civilisation of all the tribes inhabiting the shores and islands of the River Amazon. Father Vieira was charged with this undertaking, and was received with enthusiastic joy by the Indians, who had learned to know the Jesuits as their true friends. More than one hundred thousand natives agreed to a treaty, binding them to embrace the faith of Jesus Christ, and "to live in perpetual peace with the Portuguese, being the friend of their friends, and the enemy of their enemies". The Europeans, however, were disappointed and annoyed that they could no longer despoil the natives and make slaves of them. Defeated avarice inflamed them with such bitter hatred of the missionaries that they forcibly placed Father Vieira and other Jesuits on board vessels bound for Lisbon, and publicly accused the order of seeking sovereign power and aggrandisement. A serious revolt of the natives followed. It may, indeed, be said that evil passions among Christians have done more to counteract missionary enterprise than the ignorance and prejudices of the savages.

In 1697 the Jesuits entered California, and at this time they were already established in Guiana and in several of the West Indian Islands. In North America the work of the Jesuits was as great and noble as it was in the southern portion of the Continent. A Protestant traveller in Canada* says:—" The devotion of the Missionaries impressed me profoundly. Great eulogiums are due to the Priests. By means of indefatigable zeal and the example of their own virtues, they have converted a race of savages. Their own excellent lives increases the respect of these pious Indians for them and for their religion." The mission to the Red Indians was going on favourably when the English intervened in 1613. In the year 1625 the Fathers Masse, John De Breboeuf, Lulemant, Rugueneau and twenty other Jesuits arrived in Canada. Over mountains and through forests, across great lakes and rivers amidst the terrible cold of an arctic winter, and under the short but great heats of summer, they laboured among the Hurons, the Algonquins, the Iroquois, and other tribes. The gospel of christian love, meekness, and humility was preached in their actions and by their words. God blessed their work and thousands were converted. Among the wild savages the knowledge and love of Jesus Christ sprang forth as fountains in the desert, fer-

* *Travels in Canada and Voyage to Hudson's Bay*, by Long. A French translation has been published.

tilising and changing all around. Towns were founded at Conception, St. Ignatius, St. Francis Xavier, St. Joseph and St Mary. North America like Japan and China was specially a country of martyrdom. When the Hurons submitted to Christianity the Iroquois attacked them. In 1643 Father Jaques and Brother Renè Goupil were quietly travelling along one of the great rivers escorted by canoes, in which were the neophytes of the new religion, when suddenly ferocious bands of Iroquois who had been in ambush, rushed forth and seized the Missionaries. After having mangled and lacerated their bodies they led them as a derisive show from village to village. Brother Goupil died with the utmost fortitude, while Father Jaques was saved by the Dutch after he had been able to despatch a letter to the French Governor warning him of an intended surprise on the part of the savages. He adds in his letter " I have baptised more than sixty persons here, several of whom have gone to heaven. This is my only consolation—that and the will of God, to which I submit mine." About this time two hundred English families established Maryland for the purpose of enjoying freedom of religion. They were accompanied by four Jesuits —Fathers Andrew White, John Althani, Brothers Knowles and Thomas Gervase.

An American Protestant writer of considerable ability and success (Parkman—*The Jesuits in North America*) tells us that "The Jesuits gained the confidence and good will of the Huron population. Their patience, their kindness, their intrepidity, their manifest disinterestedness, the blamelessness of their lives, and the tact which, in the utmost fervour of their zeal, never failed them, had won the hearts of the wayward savages, and chiefs of distant villages came to urge that they would make their abode with them." Again

he says, " When we see them, in the gloomy February of
1637, and the gloomier months that followed, toiling on
foot from one infected town to another (the small-pox was
raging everywhere), wading through the sodden snow, under
the bare and dripping forests, drenched with incessant rains,
till they descried at length through the storm the clustered
dwellings of some barbarous hamlet,—when we see them
entering, one after another, these wretched abodes of misery
and darkness, and all for one sole end, the baptism of the
sick and dying, we may smile at the futility of the object,
but we must needs admire the self-sacrificing zeal with
which it was pursued " (p. 98). The same writer says, " No-
where is the power of courage, faith, and an unflinching
purpose more strikingly displayed than in the record of these
missions. The Jesuits had borne all that the human frame
seems capable of bearing—mutilation, tortures, famine, and
the menace of death in its most frightful forms, at every hour
of the day and night. Their zeal never flagged, their courage
never failed. An intense and unquenchable fervour urged
them on." Bancroft, in his history of the United States,
speaks of these Missionaries in the very highest terms, and
it is certain that no more devoted men ever carried the
gospel of Jesus Christ to savage nations. Among the Cana-
dian Missionaries Father Jean de Brebœuf stands forth as a
conspicuous figure. Parkman, the traveller, styles him " the
Ajax of the Huron mission, its truest hero and its greatest
martyr ". Even the ferocious Iroquois were astounded at
his fortitude under most severe torments. His whole life
was a victory over the flesh, and he possessed a courage un-
conscious of fear yet redeemed from rashness by a cool and
vigorous judgment. After having been a thousand times a
martyr he was at last tortured to death, and thus finished a

most glorious course run for the salvation of the savages of North America. Another Jesuit Father, named Garnier, was a saint whose life of self-denial merited the final crown of martyrdom which he received from the Iroquois. He would walk thirty or forty miles in the hottest day to baptise a dying Indian at a time when the country was infested with enemies. Speaking of his death Mr Parkman says, "Thus died Charles Garnier, the favourite child of wealthy and noble parents, nursed in Parisian luxury and ease. His life and death are his best eulogy. Brebœuf was the lion of the Huron mission, and Garnier was the lamb ; but the lamb was as fearless as the lion." To show the undaunted character of these men we have only to read how Joseph Marie Chaumanot, a martyr only in desire, accepted toils and sufferings before which the vulgar vanity of the greatest military heroes would have quailed. On one occasion a warrior rushed forward like a madman, drew his bow and aimed the arrow at Chaumanot. Death was imminent but the Jesuit Father calmly and fixedly looked at the savage, and with full faith and confidence commended himself to St. Michael. "Without doubt," he writes, "this great Archangel saved us, for almost immediately the fury of the warrior was appeased."

The traveller Parkman, writing of the Indians of North America, says truly that no race perhaps ever offered greater difficulties to those labouring for its improvement. Yet the Jesuits converted nearly the entire Huron nation, not to speak now of other northern tribes. Regarding the influence and character of these missions the same impartial and non-Catholic writer already quoted (Parkman) eloquently says : "What was their prayer ? It was a petition for the forgiveness and conversion of their enemies, the Iroquois. Those

who know the intensity and tenacity of an Indian's hatred
will see in this something more than a change from one super-
stition to another. An idea has been presented to the mind
of the savage, *to which he had previously been an utter stranger.*
This is the most remarkable record of success in the whole
body of the Jesuit *Relations;* but it is very far from being
the only evidence that, in teaching the dogmas and observ-
ances of the Roman Church, the missionaries taught also
the morals of Christianity. When we look for the result of
these missions, we soon become aware that the influence of
the French and the Jesuits *extended far beyond the circle of
converts.* It eventually modified and softened the manners
of many unconverted tribes. In the wars of next century
we do not often find those examples of diabolic atrocity with
which the earlier annals are crowded. The savage was a
savage still, but not so often a devil. . . . . Thus Philip's
war in New Zealand, cruel as it was, was less ferocious than
it would have been. . . . . Yet it was to French priests and
colonists that the change is chiefly to be ascribed " (pp. 319,
20).

CHAPTER IV.

Jesuit missions in Japan. A Japanese Henry VIII. Inhuman persecutions. Missions in China. Father Ricci. Tonquin and Cochin China. The dispute about Chinese ceremonies. Bulls of Benedict XIV. Missions in India, Philippines, &c.

WE must now refer to the Jesuit missions in Japan, China, and the East Indies.

About the middle of the sixteenth century the seed of the Gospel sown by Francis Xavier in Japan bore its fruits in thousands of Christians, who firmly professed the faith of Jesus Christ. The son of Civandono, King of Bungo, and also the King of Aruna had been converted and baptised. A handsome stone church was erected in the capital of the kingdom in 1576. Although this nation produced many martyrs, its people generally were fickle, and, although gifted with great powers of imitation, were little to be trusted, and certainly were far inferior in intelligence to the inhabitants of Northern Europe. In 1577 thirteen Fathers were sent to Japan, accompanied by Brother Louis Almeida, who devoted his fortune to the mission, and became a catechist and preacher. It is noticeable that, so far from the Jesuits hastily administering baptism, they were, on the contrary, extremely careful only to accord it after long perseverance had proved the worthiness of the recipients. The Queen of Joscimond even was refused the sacrament when she expressed a desire for its reception. On this occasion one of the Fathers remarked, in reply to the complaint of the King, "You see, Prince, how widely our law differs from that of the Bonzes. Where is the one among them who, at the request of a King like you, would refuse to initiate the Queen in the mysteries of his sect? But the Christians pursue a different course when the eternal salvation of the soul is in question. The Queen is not sufficiently experienced in the practice of our holy religion." In the year 1579 there were in Japan twenty-nine Jesuits and one hundred thousand Christians. The work of conversion went on unceasingly, and so was it blessed by God that, in 1587, there were three hundred thousand Catholics in Japan, including several kings, princes, and men of high rank. But a fearful change was about to take place, and it is a coincidence that, while almost at the same period the gratification of lust was the cause of the English Reformation, so in Japan did the same cause operate to effect a similar result, in the form of a disastrous religious revolution. In accordance with custom, a Pagan Bonze was deputed to seek the most handsome woman of the empire for presentation to the Emperor. Two young and beautiful Christian women declined "this great honour," in accordance with the dictates of their religion, and this was at once represented as a grave insult to the Prince. It was represented that if the "Bonzes of Europe" were allowed to proceed in this way the will of the Prince would be subjected to their influence. As a side issue, great stress was laid upon the frightful crime which Europeans constantly committed in eating the flesh of the ox. The Emperor, enraged that the religion of Jesus Christ should dare to interfere with the gratification of his lust, immediately commanded his Prime Minister to abjure Christianity, and, upon his refusing, condemned him to exile and confiscated his entire possessions. Not only did this Japanese Sir Thomas More suffer in person, but his aged father with his wife and children were also reduced to poverty. Then the terrible edict was issued that the Jesuits were to leave Japan within twenty days. The exercise of the Christian religion was strictly prohibited, and it was solemnly announced that the system of the European Bonzes was of "the evil one," because they used oxen for their food and destroyed the pagan idols. Every Japanese Christian who refused to abjure Jesus Christ was condemned to death. No fewer than one hundred and seventeen Jesuits met at a place named Firando, and the Apostles of Japan determined rather to die than to abandon their mission. Seventy churches were burned or otherwise destroyed, and further acts of violence would have been committed but for fear of a revolt among the Christians, who now formed an important section of the community.

The first Japanese Christian martyrs put to death were Joachim Namura and Joram Nacama. Thousands of Christians now enthusiastically declared themselves, and even kings solicited baptism. While these events were occurring, Father Alexander Valignani had been absent at Rome with the Ambassadors from Japan. So soon as he became aware of the Christian persecution he requested the Portuguese Viceroy of the Indies to appoint him Ambassador to Japan, as he was aware of a law by which if any one condemned to death could obtain admittance to the Emperor's presence, he himself and his family and friends

would be immediately pardoned. This plan had the desired
effect. The Ruler of Japan was propitiated, and the Jesuits
were allowed to remain in the Empire—at the same time,
both preaching and public worship were prohibited. The
Missionaries were therefore compelled from this time to
carry on the work of their Apostolate secretly. When war
was declared against the Corea, about the beginning of the
seventeenth century, a Christian general was appointed to
command the Japanese troops, and he took with him two
Jesuit Fathers, so that it was in this way that Christianity
first entered that country.

There was great reason to fear that Christianity would be
entirely stamped out in Japan, but the Jesuits there, as in
England, tenaciously adhered, in spite of torments and of
death, to the post of honour which had been allotted to
them. The Father-General asked the Pope to obtain a
reinforcement from other orders, but His Holiness, in a
Bull dated January 28, 1585, declared himself opposed to
this proposal. Philip II. of Spain called the attention of his
governors in the East to this decision, and expressly forbade
any missionaries other than Jesuits to enter Japan. After
the lapse of several years, it was rumoured that the Jesuits
had ceased to exist in that Empire. A new embassy was
therefore sent by the Viceroy of the Philippine Islands,
comprising five Franciscan Fathers. One of the first persons that these monks met in Japan was Father Organtini,
who informed them that the number of his order in the
island was no fewer than one hundred and twenty-six. In
February, 1596, several Jesuits came out to assist their
brethren, and in the month of July in the same year a
French ship, with a valuable cargo, was wrecked on the
coast of Japan. Some maps and charts were discovered in

the wreck, and the Spanish pilot was foolish enough to inform a Japanese nobleman that the countries indicated in them belonged to the King of Spain. When asked how his sovereign had made himself master of so many countries, the answer was, "By force of arms and of religion. Our priests go first and prepare the way by converting the people, and, when Christianity predominates, on our arrival the conquest is but mere child's play." These words were quickly reported to the Emperor, who immediately ordered that all the Christian priests and teachers should be seized. This was done at once, and they were sentenced to be crucified at Nangesaki. Then occurred a scene such as those which proved the divinity of the Christian religion under Nero and Domitian. Father Paul Miki was unable to restrain his excessive joy, and threw himself into the arms of each of the Franciscan Fathers, thanking them with lively expressions of joy for the happiness which their teaching had bestowed upon him. These holy martyrs died the same death as Jesus Christ, and welcomed their fate with so much joy that the Emperor was completely deceived and disappointed. After the lapse of some time the decree of death to Christians was temporarily suspended under the influence of Father Valignani, Provincial of the Jesuits. Shortly afterwards the ruler of Japan died a pagan, although the most pressing, constant, and able efforts had been used for his conversion. The heir to the crown was a child of six years of age, and the Regent appointed declared in favour of Christianity. The Church prospered. In 1599 there was a very large number Christians, and so great was the work that Father Bueza, like St. Francis Xavier, had frequently to get his arms supported when administering the sacrament of baptism. There was an excellent seminary and numerous native priests, while one of the most important establishments was an institution for the reception of pagan children whose parents were so poor that they would have put them to death.

A dreadful change was about to take place. In 1612 an English Protestant captain, out of enmity to the Spaniards, alarmed the easily awakened jealousy of the Japanese authorities. He stated that Spain had determined to take possession of Japan, and that the Jesuits were merely spies sent before to pave the way. He informed them that the Fathers of the order taught a false religion, and had been on that account expelled from England, Germany, Poland, and Holland. The Dutch joined the English in urging upon the Japanese the desirability of expelling the Jesuits. The country would be benefited they said, as *their* object was merely trade. They succeeded only too well. In 1613 the persecution became terrible—seventeen hundred martyrs sealed their confession with their blood. No fewer than one hundred and seventeen Jesuits, as well as members of other orders, and seven native Priests were banished. Twenty-six Jesuits and a few other missionaries remained in Japan. A frightful time of penal laws and of cruel persecution followed. The edicts of Elizabeth in England became those of the Emperor of Japan. It was death to harbour a missionary, but unlike the hunted Priests of Britain the Jesuits were at first able to preach the faith openly, as a large portion of the people boldly declared in their favour. Soon, however, they were compelled to travel dressed as merchants. In this garb Fathers Jerome de Angelis and Carvalho passed through the country, consoling, fortifying and encouraging the Christians, and lifting many up from paganism to the light of truth. Once blood commenced to flow it seemed only to urge the persecutors to further excesses, and the Protestant writer Kaempfer, in his *History of Japan* (Vol. II., p. 166), thus speaks of the terrible revolution against Christianity so well planted by Jesuits, and so well watered with the blood of martyrs. He styles the persecution in Japan one of the greatest mentioned in history. In one year alone 20,570 people were put to death for the crime of professing the Christian religion. When Father Spinola was summoned before a governor and asked, "Why he dared to reside in the Empire contrary to the command of the Emperor?" He replied, "I ask you in my turn what you would decide to do if a King of Japan gave you certain instructions, and the Emperor, who is master over all the Kings in Japan, issued contrary orders. Who would you be bound to obey? Our position is similar. The Sovereign of heaven and earth has sent us here to preach the gospel. The Emperor Xogun gives us certain instructions. To whom must we submit?" Spinola and two other missionaries were cast into a loathsome dungeon, and when they saw the dreadful place of their imprisonment immediately intoned the "Te Deum". When Father Leonard Kimura had been found innocent of murder, for which he was tried by a court at Nangasacki, he was asked previous to leaving the Court whether he could inform against any Jesuit—"I know only of one," was the reply, "and I am ready to deliver him up". This news was received with enthusiasm, and soldiers were offered to make the important capture. "Do not take so much trouble," replied the Father, "you have no need of troublous search or an armed force, the person whom I know is before you, it is myself." After three years of captivity, this noble missionary was burned alive with several other martyrs.

Although there was no Tower of London in Japan, with its "scavenger's daughter," "thumb screws," and other tortures, the Governor of Nangasacki was sufficiently ingenious. He constructed a large cage, in which the prisoners were cramped up and exposed both to the cold of winter and to the heat of summer. This became a house of novices of the Society of Jesus, as many Japanese Christians imprisoned in it were at their earnest request admitted to the order. Father Charles Spinola and Father Fernandez distinguished themselves here by their example and instructions. In spite of the terrible persecution and edicts against those who should dare to shelter Jesuits, we find that in 1621 five Fathers arrived by sea, habited as merchants. On the 10th of September, 1622, twenty-four religious, who had been shut up in the cages of Omura, were condemned to be burned alive. Father Spinola marched at their head with seven novices to a place called the Sacred Mount. Thirty-one native Christians were present, who were also condemned to die, and, on the invitation of their leader, both bands intoned the psalm, "Praise the Lord, ye children, praise ye the name of the Lord". Then the intrepid missionary spoke aloud, and asked whether it was likely that men who rejoiced to die in this manner were people who merely worked for the purpose of making Japan subject to some earthly kingdom. "It is your true happiness we desire. These flames, which now attack our feet and will soon envelop us, are for us the dawning light of an eternal repose." The signal for execution was given and the martyrs were released.

On the 19th September, 1622, Fathers Costanzo, Oto, and Novarra expired in the flames lighted for the destruction of the Catholic religion in Japan. On the 1st of

November following, Denis Fugixima and Peter Onizuka followed on the same fiery path to heaven. It would be impossible to give full details of this awful persecution. Some of the most insidious and dreadful tortures that can be imagined were adopted in order that the Christians might be deprived of the priceless crown of martyrdom. Not only was the flesh of victims slowly wrenched from their bones, the nails of their fingers and toes torn off, their legs, arms, noses, and ears pierced with sharp instruments of iron, but they were thrown into ditches filled with vipers or into pools of the most vile putrefying matter. Sometimes the martyrs were extended naked over braziers filled with fire, and the least movement or cry was ostentatiously declared to be an act of apostasy; sometimes hot vases had to be held, and if the hand shook this was taken to mean an act of obedience to the edicts of the Emperor ; sometimes the victims were suspended over a putrid sewer, with their right hands close to a bell, which if touched in the slightest would immediately sound the signal both of their apostasy and release. Kaempfer tells us that the pagans, not being able to prove the new converts wrong by argument, made use of the powerful reasoning of fire, sword, gibbets, crosses, and torments. In spite of this treatment and of the frightful diversity of punishments used, the martyrs suffered cheerfully and victoriously. It is as lamentable as it is true that the Dutch and English traders caused and fomented this sanguinary persecution. Blind hatred to the Jesuits and to the Catholic Church, joined to the jealous desire of trade monopoly, were the sources of torrents of blood and the means of banishing Christianity from Japan. Over and over again the Jesuits sent missionaries, but they were only sent to be sacrificed. A Dutch Protestant named Reyer

Gysbert, who was at Nangasacki for several years prior to 1629, says that the number of Christian martyrs was incalculable. As it was said of Augustine in relation to his mother, St. Monica—" The subject of so many tears cannot be lost "—so may we hope that it can be said of Japan that the earth which has been so saturated with the blood of martyrs cannot be lost permanently to Christianity. Its time has yet to come.

It seems as if the blessings intended for Japan were transferred to China. The latter country was the promised land of St. Francis Xavier which he never entered, but on whose confines he expired. Almost at the same time that this great Saint drew his last breath on the sea-beach of an island in the eastern seas Matthew Ricci was born in Italy. This great Jesuit missionary was destined to be the pioneer of Christianity in China, and we find him at the beginning of the seventeenth century successfully identifying himself with the manners and customs of those he desired to convert. He became all things to all men that he might gain them to Christ. Habited in the costume of the learned he proved to the most learned Chinese that he was their superior in the knowledge of various branches of natural philosophy —specially including astronomy. After many difficulties Father Ricci obtained an introduction to the Emperor at Pekin and presented him with a clock for which a suitable tower was built. Pictures of our Saviour and of the Blessed Virgin Mary were placed in the Palace. . The favour of the Court enabled the Jesuit to preach Jesus Christ to the greatest people of the land. Many Mandarins were baptised and their example and influence were of consequence. A novitiate was established at Pekin in 1607, and when Father Ricci died at his post, three years afterwards, he had the consolation of knowing that the work of his apostolate had been singularly blessed. Crowds followed his body to the grave, and the Emperor caused a Catholic church to be erected over the spot where the mortal remains reposed of one of the greatest, wisest, and most learned men China had ever known. In this great empire it was absolutely necessary to have able men of great intelligence and knowledge as missionaries, and the Jesuit order proved itself fully equal to the situation. The Holy See had authorised a wide and wise latitude interdicting only that which is contrary to faith or morals, but as some of the Fathers had scruples of conscience with reference to the toleration of several customs, the Provincial called them together at Pekin, when, in a general assembly, a common course of action was decided upon. To attend this some of the Fathers had to walk eight hundred leagues.

Father Adam Schall gained great favour and influence in China on account of his abilities as a mathematician. In correcting the calendar of the Celestial Empire he took care to abolish lucky and unlucky days, and was able to convince the people of the soundness of his views. Christianity spread rapidly and labourers were always in demand. In applying to the General for reinforcements Father Diaz wrote :—" I ask you for twenty, and it would not be too many, if all, by a special blessing of heaven, should arrive at Macao in safety; but it is not uncommon for about half of them to die on the way. It is necessary therefore to send twenty a year to depend on ten."   .

Three Dominican monks who had gone to China to assist the Jesuits became scandalised by the toleration extended to national customs and practices. They had not penetrated thoroughly the ideas of the people, and looking only at the surface naturally formed an opinion which a profound study of the question would have modified or changed. They reported to the Archbishop of Manilla that the Christians were permitted to prostrate themselves before an idol, to render superstitious worship to their ancestors, and to offer sacrifice to Confucius. The entire subject was laid before the Pope. The Dominican monks, more zealous than discreet, publicly informed the Chinese people that Confucius and all the sovereigns of China were damned, and that the Jesuit Fathers betrayed the faith by concealing these truths. They were immediately dragged before the authorities. Some time afterwards the Archbishop of Manilla and the Bishop of Zebu wrote to Urban VIII. that being fully informed of the habits and customs of the Chinese tolerated by the Jesuits, they justified those religious, approved of their proceedings, and applauded their zeal.

In Tonquin and Cochin China Christianity spread rapidly under the direction of the Society of Jesus. In 1624 Father Alexander de Rhodes arrived there and soon so identified himself with the people as to gain their affection, confidence, and friendship. He was subsequently so very successful as to alarm the Ruler of Cochin China, who condemned the missionary to banishment and persecuted the converts ; but Father de Rhodes wrote :—"I was the only Priest in the whole country. I was not callous enough to leave thirty thousand Christians without a Pastor. I withdrew from the court and kept myself concealed, generally remaining in the day time in a boat, with eight of my catechists, and at night I went among the Christians, who secretly assembled in their houses." Some years afterwards—in 1649—Father De Rhodes was sent to Europe, and travelled through Persia, Media, Natolia and Armenia in order to make himself acquainted with the possibilities of missionary enterprise in these countries.

Pope Innocent X. received him with fatherly affection and was desirous of appointing him to the Bishopric of Cochin China, but this devoted missionary could not be induced to accept such a dignity.

In spite of the civil war which desolated China the Jesuit missions continued to flourish. Siding neither with the Tartar invaders nor with the Chinese people, the missionaries devoted themselves earnestly to the conversion of both. One of the Emperors, named Jun Lie, who had become a Christian, retained at his Court Fathers Cœffler and Michael Boym. The Empress, his wife, took the name of Helen, and when she gave birth to a son in the year 1650 he was baptised "Constantine". At Pekin, Father Adam Schall continued to be esteemed, revered, and listened to because of his learning and virtue. The effect of his teaching and example was most marked, and most beneficial. The Tartar invasion succeeded, and the Christian Emperor, Jun Lié, was defeated and killed. The Empress was made prisoner and taken to Pekin. The new Ruler was a man of liberal and enlightened views who commanded that the Doctors of the divine law who had come from the West should be respected throughout all the provinces of the Empire. Personally he lost the grace of conversion in consequence of his disinclination to abandon sensual habits. He died prematurely and left an infant as his successor. Previous to his decease, the Emperor had forced the title of Mandarin upon Father Adam Schall and had appointed him to take charge of his son's education. At this time the Jesuits possessed one hundred and fifty-one churches and thirty-eight residences in China, and they had written in the Chinese language no fewer than one hundred and thirty books on religion, one hundred and three on mathematics, and one hundred and five on natural philosophy and morals. We cannot wonder that the Bonzes were filled with envy and indignation, and that they sought every possible opportunity of making war against Christianity. It was unfortunate that the sway of an experienced and able monarch had been changed for the woes connected with the rule of a child. The minds of the regents were easily poisoned, and as a result the missionaries were ordered to Pekin and there condemned to perpetual banishment. Nineteen Jesuits were sent to the prisons of Canton. Father Schall was condemned to be cut to pieces, but was liberated at the earnest solicitation of many people thankful for his generosities and sensible of his goodness. This great father did not long survive. He died on the 15th August, 1666, at the age of 79, after having spent more than 44 years in the evangelisation, instruction, and edification of the people of China.

The Jesuits in China had to undergo most trying experiences, encounter constant dangers, and exercise consummate prudence. God Almighty, however, specially blessed their labours, and their success was most marked and extraordinary. In May 1688 the Emperor Kang Hi sent Father Francis Gerbellon, accompanied by Father Pereira, as ambassador to the Czar of Russia. So successful was this mission that on its completion the Jesuit was solemnly clothed in Imperial robes, and the Emperor took the order into his special favour. These honours, privileges, and marks of good will were all used " to the greater glory of God," for the advancement of His Kingdom by the conversion of souls.

The eighteenth century brought with it serious religious troubles to China. In June, 1706, the Cardinal de Tournon, legate of the Holy See, who was received by the Emperor of China, insisted upon forbidding Christians to observe civil ceremonies in honour of Confucius and the ancients. The Emperor in reply prohibited the Jesuits from teaching in opposition to legalised customs. Upon this the Legate published an edict positively forbidding Christians to give to God the name of "Xanti" or "Tien," and to render Confucius and the ancients the accustomed honours. The absolute monarch of China was so enraged that he delivered over the Cardinal Legate to his Portugese enemies, who confined him in a dungeon at Macao. Father Gerbellon could not appease the Emperor's anger, and died amidst these troubles. He had ever treated the Legate with the utmost respect, and therefore evidently lost the confidence of the Government. The Viceroy of India, the Archbishop of Goa, and the Bishop of Macao prohibited Cardinal de Tournon from exercising his Legatine authority in the Portuguese colonies, and both the Bishop and the Captain-General of Macao were excommunicated by him. He expired in his dungeon at Macao on the 8th of June, 1710, at the age of forty-two years. It is necessary to explain that in China, the Jesuits, thoroughly understanding the customs of the people, believed that they were right in tolerating certain practices which they considered were purely civil. In a letter to Pope Clement XI., they declare that they heartily wish that it were in their power to abolish all the pagan rites and ceremonies in which there was the smallest suspicion of evil—" but for fear by that severity of barring the entrance to the gospel, we are obliged, after the example of the Holy Fathers of the primitive Church, to tolerate the ceremonies of the gentiles which are purely civil in such a way that with as little danger as possible we may by degrees substitute Christian ceremonies for them". They asked the Holy See to declare in their favour. Cardinal Tournon was even-

tually sent as Legate with the result we have stated. This
ecclesiastic began by raising a terrible storm against himself
among the Portuguese, by forbidding various local customs.
These people declared that he exceeded his instructions and
went beyond his authority, and we have already seen the
sad fate of the fearless Legate. The Jansenists in Europe
did not hesitate to stigmatise the Jesuits in China as murderers of the Cardinal. It is observable that the great
Dignitary of the Church had not, and could not have had,
that profound knowledge of the difficult subject of Chinese
ceremonial possessed by the missionaries who had lived for
many years in the country. Leibnitz, who on this subject
is certainly impartial, and was one of the ablest and keenest
thinkers of his time, states that he regards the Emperor's
declaration that the customs were not religious as of very
great weight, and considers that the missionaries were not
wrong in the course that they pursued. They certainly, however, were mistaken in some respects, and the Holy See in
September, 1710, distinctly and definitely condemned some
of the ceremonies which the Jesuits had not forbidden. The
Society, as in duty bound, thoroughly and completely submitted. The Bull *Ex illa die* of the 19th March, 1715, put
an end to all difficulties and forced the missionaries to break
entirely with Chinese ceremonies of an objectionable character.

The Emperor Kiang Hi died in 1722, and his successor
Yong Tching, proved a deadly enemy to Christianity.
Princes of the royal family who had become Catholics were
despoiled of their titles and honours, exiled, and threatened
with death. All missionaries, except Jesuits, were ordered
to Macao, and the latter only found grace because of their
usefulness in drawing up maps and giving scientific instruc-

tion. Their position was indeed singular. In other countries they were always the first to suffer, but in China their learning formed an ægis of protection. On the 6th October, 1726, Father Gaubel writes from Pekin :—" The Jesuits have here three large churches ; they yearly baptise three thousand infants exposed to suffer death. So far as I can judge from the number of confessions and communions, there are three thousand Christians here who frequent the sacraments. In this number there are only four or five petty mandarins—the rest are poor people. . . . Besides the Christian princes of whose fervour and misfortunes you have heard, there are two other princes who have renounced their dignities and employments for the purpose of becoming Christians. . . . The Emperor does not love religion ; the great people therefore avoid it. We seldom appear at the palace, but we are wanted for the tribunal of mathematics, for Russian affairs, and for the scientific instruments and other things which come from Europe." This Father goes on to say that in the towns of Chang-Nan and of Song-Kiang, in the province of Nankin, there are more than one hundred thousand Christians. He tells us that all the missionaries had to work secretly, and that a single accusation against a concealed Priest brought to the Emperor, would ruin all. He estimates the total Christian population of China and Tartary at more than three hundred thousand, and is of opinion that if it were not for past disputes their number would have been five millions. Father Gaubil was a distinguished member of the French and Russian Academies, and did much for science as a means of working for Christianity. The Jesuits in China were distinguished astronomers, mathematicians, annalists, geographers, physicians, painters, and mechanicians. It was absolutely necessary that they should excel in science to retain any footing in the empire. Men of great ability, piety, and devotion gave their lives for Jesus Christ. Taking one as a type of many, it is thus that Father Parrenin is referred to :—"It seems that God had formed him by a special providence to be, in very difficult times, the mainstay and the soul of this mission. He had united in his own person the qualities of body and of soul, which constituted him one of the most able and most zealous workers which our Society has ever given to China— a large, well-made man of robust constitution, of venerable and majestic appearance, gifted with an extraordinary facility for acquiring languages, and endowed with penetrating judgment, and great ability."

Disputes about Chinese rites and ceremonies had exercised, as we have seen, a most prejudicial effect upon Christian missions. All doubts, questions, and opinions were finally settled by the Bulls *Ex quo singulari* and *Omnium solicitudinem*, issued by Pope Benedict XIV. in July, 1742, and September, 1744. The Jesuits, of course, submitted without reserve. Persecution followed both in India and China. In the latter country, the Mandarins, urged on by the Bonzes, pressed forward a reactionary movement which swept away missions and missionaries. Banishment and death by the sword was the fate of devoted evangelists except in Pekin, where Christianity took shelter under the banners of science, and several Jesuit Fathers were enabled to keep up the sacred flame of religion while directing mathematical, mechanical, and industrial education.

The great work of evangelisation commenced so successfully by St. Francis Xavier in the East Indies was prosecuted indefatigably, not only in Hindostan but in the Isles of the

Eastern Archipelago. In the Moluccas, the faithful were assaulted in the eighteenth century by a specially fierce persecution, in which, as usual, the Mahommedans proved themselves the deadly enemies of Christianity. This system of antichrist has always been the most bitter foe of the faith, and the followers of the false prophet so mingle religious fanaticism with the indulgence of their passions that they have been generally extremely successful among demoralised nations, where sensuality completely prevails. Father Mascarenas was able to save from Islamism the kingdom of Siokon, in the island of Mindanao; that of Manado, in the island of Celebes; and that of Sanghir, near the Philippines.

Looking back at the history of the Jesuits in Hindostan, we find that very soon after the establishment of the first missions, Father Rudolphus Aquaviva was massacred at Salsette, and that the Grand Mogul, Akbar, manifested the deepest sorrow when he heard of his martyrdom. To this great ruler another missionary was sent during 1595, in the person of Father Geronimo Xavier, nephew of the great apostle. Success followed his labours, and multitudes were converted. Akbar was too sensual to become a Christian, but after his death three princes of his house were converted. Christianity became then permanently established in India, and has ever since continued to exist. The missions of the present day may be said to flourish exceedingly. The Order of Jesus planted and watered—God has given the increase.

CHAPTER V.

Missions in the North of Europe. Father Possevin. Lutheran persecutors. Queen Christina. Germany. Don John of Austria. The Low Countries. War and pestilence. Persecutions and martyrdoms in Germany. Awful persecutions in England and Ireland. Cromwell and the Puritans. Infamous plot of Titus Oates. Persecutions in France. Foul calumnies. Jansenism. The Plague.

IT is now necessary to consider the progress of the Society in the various kingdoms of Europe. Towards the close of the sixteenth century, Father Possevin had proceeded to Sweden and there won not only the love and veneration of Catholics, but the esteem of the Lutherans. Having left several Fathers in charge, he proceeded to give an account of his mission to the Pope. At this time, Ivan IV., Czar of Russia, sent an ambassador to the Holy See in order to beg that a legate might be sent to mediate between himself and the King of Poland. Father Possevin was chosen and instructed to specially stipulate for toleration, and that a free passage might be given through the Russian territories to missionaries for India, Tartary, and China. A treaty of peace was the consequence, and there is no doubt that this satisfactory result was entirely attributable to the ability, patience, and goodness of the Papal legate. The

Pope was so satisfied that he desired to use the talents of
Father Possevin against the Arians, Anabaptists, Lutherans,
and Calvinists, who had reduced Livonia and Transylvania
to a deplorable condition. Having received the blessing of
the General, this Father proceeded on foot from Rome to
Poland, carried on controversies with the greatest success,
and was enabled to establish colleges and a seminary. A
man who had proved himself able to elucidate the most
difficult propositions, and to solve the most intricate questions with clearness and rapidity, was justly considered to be
a very competent arbiter. We cannot, therefore, be surprised
that when Poland and Germany submitted their differences
to the mediation of the Pope, they desired that His Holiness
might be represented by Father Possevin. The rage of the
heretics and schismatics waxed so intense that the Father
General (Aquaviva), became alarmed at the European
celebrity of one of his children. He begged that His Holiness would withdraw him from the political mission with
which he had been entrusted, saying : " The Society was
founded solely for the glory of God and of His Church, and
not to serve the political designs of sovereigns. To employ
our Fathers in such negotiations is to expose them to the
danger of acquiring a taste for the world totally incompatible
with their vows ; it is launching them upon a perilous sea
. . . . It is not for Possevin that I fear the plaudits of
the world ; his virtue is known to me. But there is danger
for the Society, and your Holiness must preserve us from
it." Father Possevin was recalled, and left his arduous
diplomatic duties to resume those of his apostolical mission.
He revivified the faith, combated heresies, founded colleges,
and worthily received the title of Apostle of the North.

We have seen Calvinists killing Jesuits on the high seas—

7

thinking that they did God a service.   We will now see
Lutherans persecuting them to death in Poland and Russia.
King Sigismund desired to found a new college of the Jesuits
at Cracow, but his project was opposed with the utmost
jealousy by the professors of the existing university, who
went so far as to declare that the Fathers of the Order of
Jesus were "skilled in a thousand artifices, and are instructed
to feign simplicity".   The best reply to this was to carry
out the project.   A revolution was then threatened, and the
Lutherans took up arms, but were quickly and efficiently
repressed.   Then with extraordinary malignity they published
abroad that "the city was inundated with the blood of the
innocent which the Jesuits caused to be spilt ; but the
Fathers, not being content with the slaughter, employed executioners, whose arms grew tired, and who, touched with
pity, at length refused to continue the massacre".   This
new "Massacre of the Innocents" so delighted the enemies
of the order that copies of this infamous calumny were
eagerly circulated and readily believed.

In 1621 the Swedish Lutherans forced the city of Riga to
capitulate, and the expulsion of the Jesuits was one of the
conditions insisted upon.   Gustavus Adolphus expelled
them from Venden, but was shortly afterwards defeated by
Corvin Gosiewski, the Palatine of Smolensk, who founded a
college of Jesuits at Dunemunde in thanksgiving for his
victory.   "If you be expelled from one city, pass to another."
The loss of one nation is the gain of another.   The Jesuits,
expelled from Poland and Sweden by the Lutherans, were
warmly received in Hungary, where Father Peter Pasmany
had performed such work as to be styled an apostle.   He
was so valued and beloved that the strongest pressure was
brought to bear on the Holy See, in order that he might be

appointed Archbishop of Gran. The result was an order which had to be obeyed, and the humble religious was obliged, against the will of the Father-General and his own inclinations, to take upon him the heavy burden of this dignity.

In the year 1650, Don Jose Pinto Pereira arrived in Sweden as Portuguese Ambassador, accompanied by an interpreter named Don Antonio Macedo. The latter was a priest of the Society of Jesus, sent in order to the instruction of the Queen (Christina) in the Catholic religion. This able Princess had seen the aridity and falsity of Lutheranism which she was forced openly to profess, and, like all great thinkers, perceived clearly that if Christianity were correct the Catholic religion was the only true one. The General of the Jesuits, in response to the Queen's request, sent Fathers Casati and Molinio who had to be introduced as Italian gentlemen on a tour. "Thus," says a Protestant historian, "in the royal palace of Gustavus Adolphus, envoys from Rome met the daughter of that monarch, who was the most zealous defender of Protestantism, to treat with her on the subject of her conversion to Catholicism." She was happily convinced, abdicated, and was received into the Church at Innspruck on the 5th of November, 1655.

The successful labours of Fathers Jay and Bobadilla in Germany have already been referred to, as well as the distinguished part which the Society was commanded to take in connection with the deliberations of the Council of Trent. The apostleship of Father Canisius was productive of wonderful fruit. He went from diocese to diocese, extending aid and consolation while refuting and uprooting heresy, and confirming thousands in the Catholic faith. The fathers of the order in the north of Europe signally distinguished themselves, and, in becoming ardent and successful champions of the faith, exposed themselves and their order to the malignant shafts of calumny. In the conflict with heresy, error, and sin they have been the most exposed troops of the Church, and have therefore received quite an extra portion of the fire of hatred from unscrupulous enemies.

Don Juan of Austria, the heroic conqueror of Lepanto, was known to be sincerely attached to the Jesuits, and when in 1576 it was announced at Antwerp that the King of Spain had appointed him to be Governor of the Netherlands, an infamous conspiracy was at once attempted against the fathers of the order. It was rumoured that they were traitors to the people, and had converted their college into an arsenal. Experience proves that any falsehood against the Society will be readily believed by their enemies. An endeavour was made to break open the doors of their house in Antwerp and to set it on fire, but fortunately the rioters were thwarted by the authorities. At the same time and hour a similar attempt was made at Liege. When Don John assumed the reins of power he discovered the Protestant intrigues, and desired to punish the leaders, but was dissuaded from doing so by the intercession of Father Bandoin de l'Ange, the Provincial of the Jesuits in Belgium, who in this manner complied with the scriptural precept of returning good for evil. But conciliation was soon found impossible. Heresy and rebellion went hand in hand, and the Prince of Orange marched forward with a hostile army for the purpose of assisting the Protestants. Churches were profaned, houses plundered, and the country devastated. Force had to be opposed to force. Don John of Austria conquered, and peace with the States was patched up. At Antwerp an oath was required from the citizens to which the Jesuits could not loyally and conscientiously subscribe. Threats and flattery having alike proved vain, the members of the order were expelled from the town, placed on board a boat on the Scheldt, and landed at Mechlin. From Bruges and Tournay the Jesuits were expelled with violence by the Protestant ،actions which ruled there. Louvain formed an asylum, and, when the pestilence which generally followed war broke out in that town, then, with their usual extreme devotion and fearless courage, the Jesuits gave their lives for the people. Fathers Usmar Baysson, John of Haarlem, Anthony Salazar, and Elisha Heivod fell victims, and soon afterwards six other fathers died at Louvain, Douay, Liege, and Brussels when ministering to the wants of the people, stricken by pestilence. The Protestant ministers, from a prudential sense of danger, retired from the towns which the plague had visited. Within a year after these events the Jesuits were reinstated in all their colleges and schools in the low countries.

It is difficult at the present period to appreciate the intense malignant intolerance which prevailed among Protestants against Jesuits at the commencement of the seventeenth century. This passion of hatred—it cannot certainly be called by a fitter title—specially animated the Calvinists, and was rendered more intense by the triumph of the Church and of the order in France under the rule of Henry IV. At Aix-la-Chapelle an insurrection, headed by Protestants, broke out on the 5th of July, 1611. The insurgents happened to encounter three Jesuits, named Father John Fladius, Nicholas Smith, and Bartholomew Jacquinat, and immediately endeavoured to take their lives, rushing upon them, crying out that they would be avenged on Papists.   The Catholics were able at that time to rescue them, but in the middle of the ensuing night the college was successfully attacked by the Protestants, when Father Philip Bebius fell under their blows, and all the other fathers were forcibly seized and dragged to the town hall. They were about to be murdered, when a voice exclaimed that one of the priests was a Frenchman.   As there was no doubt that France would avenge the blood of one of her sons, it was resolved to restore the French Jesuit to freedom, but, when Father Jacquinat was acquainted with this resolution, he nobly replied that he would never consent to be separated from his brothers, all of whom were as innocent as he.   "We do not give you your liberty on account of your innocence, but only because you are a French subject," was the response, to which Father Jacquinat replied, " In our Society we recognise neither German nor French.   We are all brothers.   Either my brothers shall be set free with me, or I will die with them."   This checked the insurgents, and, as assistance soon arrived, the insurrection was suppressed, and the Jesuits were set at liberty.   In the same year (1611) various religious houses were sacked, profaned, and destroyed at Prague, and, on a pile of paintings, ornaments, and statues, fourteen Franciscan fathers were burnt, while a crowd of fanatics, urged on by the John Knoxes of the place and period, watched their death struggles.   Calumny has invariably been the principal weapon of the enemies of the Society, and it often succeeds in spite of being used in a very clumsy and absurd manner. A rumour was spread in Prague that three hundred soldiers, together with a magazine of warlike stores and ammunition, were concealed at the Jesuits' house.   This was a signal for its immediate plunder and destruction, and although no troops were found there, the zealous haters of popery obtained an opportunity for pillage, of which they took full advantage.

It was in 1620 that Duke Maximilian of Bavaria, who had been educated by the Jesuits, putting himself and his army under divine protection, and accompanied by eighteen fathers of the order, succeeded in routing the heretical forces of Prince Frederick, Palatine Elector, and restoring order to a distracted country. The weapons with which the Society fought were those of prayer, humility, and the energetic performance of duty. Kindness and gentleness gained thousands, but their success only inflamed the hatred of the Protestants. Not only had heresy and immorality to be fought against, but bitter jealousy and continual calumnies. In 1638 the Lutherans of Utrecht were annoyed at the conversion of their Governor, the Duke of Bouillon, and declared that the Jesuits had conspired to deliver that city to the Spaniards. Father Boddens had received the recantation of the Duke, and he was impeached as the chief conspirator. History so repeats itself that we cannot be surprised at finding plots such as that of Titus Oates in other countries than England. A very circumstantial statement was made by a soldier, but it did not, unfortunately, contain the names of Jesuits. The omission however was speedily supplied, and, by means of bribes, false evidence was obtained. The chief informer however was not able to sustain a severe cross examination, and so failed as to incur the wrath of his suborners, who caused him to be put to death. They then turned their fury upon the defenceless priests, and subjected them to inhuman tortures. Fathers Boddens, Paezman, and Notting were placed on four plates of iron, arranged crosswise, and then bound with chains mounted with steel points, which pierced their flesh, while their necks were fastened in a network of lead, furnished with a triple row of teeth. Thus placed they were surrounded by a raging fire. Scarcely had the flesh been blistered by the flames than salt, vinegar, and gunpowder were poured into their bleeding wounds. Seven lighted torches were applied to their chests, and their fingers and toes were mutilated. After twenty-two hours of torture their courage remained unexhausted. A few days were then allowed to elapse, and on their expiry, in June, 1638, these glorious martyrs were executed on the scaffold. They died praying God to pardon their murderers.

In Germany, as in other countries of Europe, the Society was the chief means under God of rolling back the tide of heresy which attained such dangerous proportions in the sixteenth century. Its great success has ever been a heinous crime in the eyes of both heretics and infidels. Many of the calumnies with which the Society has been persistently attacked can be attributed to this cause. South Germany as well as France were virtually reconquered, North Germany remained Lutheran, and is now infidel. Austria fortunately has retained the faith, and in that country the Society has received immense encouragement and support.

None of the many dangerous and sanguinary fields in which the Society has fought for Christ has been more glorious than England. From the time of Elizabeth to William of Orange, the members of the order formed the "forlorn hope" of the Church militant in its attack upon heresy. These Fathers had a double duty to perform, as they were obliged both to confirm the weak and to convert those who had fallen into error. To feed the flock of Christ with the word of God and the sacraments was their chief duty, and in all the efforts of noble self-sacrificing

lives, none can be found more edifying or more glorious
than those which show how the sons of St. Ignatius cheerfully gave their lives and spent themselves for the good of
souls in England. The record is a history of cruel calumny,
bitter torture, constant martyrdom. We have glanced at
the sufferings of the Society in the reign of Elizabeth, and
adverted to the calumnies connected with the gunpowder
plot. Nothing could have been more successful than the
action of Cecil and his confederates in the latter case. They
succeeded in bringing odium upon Catholicism, and special
odium on the heads of its foremost missionary priests.
After the death of James I., the Puritans rapidly acquired
power, and their hatred of the Church was only equalled by
their ignorance of its real doctrines. It was, of course,
contrary to law for any Jesuit to live in Britain, but in spite
of cruel laws and their awful penalties, the members of the
order remained faithful to their mission. Tortures and execu-
tions seemed but to increase their ardour. Father John
Ogilvie died cheerfully on a scaffold in Glasgow for having
dared to teach the Catholic faith in a country which gloried
in having acquired "liberty of conscience". When Father
Corby was arrested in London, the German ambassador could
have effected his exchange for a Scotch prisoner, but he
preferred martyrdom, and was executed on the 14th of
September, 1644.

Father Richard Bradley died at Manchester on the 30th
January, 1645, from the cruelties to which he was made a
victim. We see him in a dungeon loaded with chains,
deprived of light, nourishment, and exercise. What was his
crime? Merely being a Catholic priest and one of the
Order of Jesus. He neither directly nor indirectly plotted
against the State; and, indeed, had been found guilty of no

crime whatsoever. But the insensate hatred of the Catholic
Church was in no country of the earth more bitter, intense,
or unreasoning than among the Protestants of England.
The representatives of all the Catholic sovereigns, who pro-
strated themselves at the feet of Father Henry Moore, and
with tears of veneration begged his blessing, must have
looked upon the people who put him to death as ignorant
barbarians destitute both of knowledge and virtue. Twenty
days after this martyr had offered up his life on the scaffold,
Father Grose expired in his dungeon at Lincoln. In Ireland the Puritan hero, Cromwell, led the most ferocious and
blood-thirsty troops who have ever prostituted the Christian
name. Crimes of sacrilege and murder abounded. No
mercy for Papists was their motto, and priests were specially
the objects of pious hatred. The Protector doomed
to death any one who should harbour a Jesuit. Fathers
Robert Netervil, Henry Cavel, Bath, and Worthington were
discovered and executed. Father Peter Wright died the
death of a common felon on the 29th of May, 1651, and a
handsome reward was given to any one who would betray to
death a member of the detested order. A time had come
when it was openly proclaimed that to slay a Jesuit was to
do God a service. It can, indeed, be truly said that neither
the North-American Indians nor the most savage of the
African tribes have ever been more ferocious enemies of
Catholic missionaries than the self-righteous Puritans. It
must honestly, however, be admitted that as our Lord
prayed for the cruel Jews, that they might be forgiven because they knew not what they did, so can we plead for the
Puritans in consequence of their very gross ignorance of the
real doctrines of the Catholic Church. The trumpet sounds
of truth had not yet blown down the walls of that Jericho of

calumny which has always kept so many inclosed within its folds.

As Ireland was a special field of danger, it was one of those for which reinforcements were easily obtained. But, in 1651, of the members of the order in that suffering country, so many had received the crown of martyrdom that only eighteen survived. The pestilence demanded its victims of charity as well as the scaffold ; and, in attendance on the sick, Fathers Lee, Kilkenny, Walsh, Dillon, and Dowdal offered up their lives. Forests, ravines, and rocky caves were used as hiding places. Father Carolan perished from exposure to the inclemency of the weather ; and missionary life was a continued series of privations, perils, and severe sufferings. It is very difficult to adequately appreciate the intensity of the Puritan hatred to Catholicism. Certainly, neither Nero nor Diocletian was a more cruel persecutor of Christianity than Cromwell, whose thoroughness was so complete that children were not spared, but seized upon in large numbers and forcibly deported to America. There, however, the Jesuits were ready to receive them, and from first to last this noble order has done much in the new world to save from destruction the sons and daughters of Ireland—" the children of those cast out ". The death of Father Boyton, S.J., forms an apt illustration of the manner in which Puritan operations were conducted. A large number of Catholics — refugees and others — took refuge in St. Patrick's Church in Cashel, and so soon as Father Boyton heard of this he knew that they would be murdered ; and that, therefore, there was pressing need for his spiritual ministrations. He proceeded there, prepared the people for death, and was martyred with them on the 15th of June, 1649.

Father Worthington shed his blood for the faith a few days after.

History proves that a nation, like an individual, can become mad. England, unfortunately, has passed through many paroxysms of fanatical insanity. So firmly were the ignorant masses imbued with the idea that the Jesuits were base, unscrupulous plotters, that their passions were very easily aroused, and then facts, evidence, common-sense, and justice were entirely thrown to the winds. In 1678 an absurdly fictitious plot was announced to King Charles the Second. Titus Oates revealed the plans of the conspiracy, and declared that he had been the principal agent of the Jesuits. "I know all," he declared; "I have seen all. I feigned to abjure Calvinism and embrace Catholicity. I entered the Society of Jesus at the English College at Valladolid; thence I went to that of St. Omer. I knew that, under the pretext of holding a congregation in 1669, the Jesuits assembled at St. James' Palace, under the protection of His Grace the Duke of York, and that there they organised plans of conspiracy such as should strike terror into the hearts of all." For the purpose of giving confirmation to his statements, Oates implored the Lord Treasurer to intercept some letters addressed to Father Bedingfield. Unfortunately, however, for the arch-plotter the Lord Treasurer was absent, and Father Bedingfield, passing the Post-Office when the mail arrived, went in and procured his letters, of which there were five. Having opened them, he found that they purported to come from four Jesuits, but that the handwriting was not theirs. In fact the contents were clumsy forgeries, and Father Bedingfield lost no time in taking them to the Duke of York, whose confessor he was. Oates was immediately summoned to the bar of the

House of Lords in the presence of the King, and, with un-
blushing audacity, stated that "he was quite sure of what he
stated. The Jesuits, urged by the Pope and by the King of
France, desire the annihilation of Anglicanism, the assassination of the King, and also of the Duke of York, if he does
not aid them in their designs. Pere La Chaise has sent
them considerable sums of money, which have been used
by them to bribe the Scotch and Irish, in order to induce
them to join the conspirators. At Paris I saw Pere La
Chaise, who received me with open arms, and counted me
out ten thousand pounds sterling." Oates having mentioned
that he had seen Don Juan of Austria, the King requested
that he would describe him. His reply was—" He is tall,
thin, and dark". Upon this the King and the Duke of
York glanced at each other and smiled. The King then
said—

" Where did you see Pere La Chaise count out the ten
thousand pounds?"

" In the house of the Jesuits, close by the Louvre," was
the reply.

"Strange," said the King, "the Jesuits have no house
within a mile of the Louvre; and Don Juan of Austria is
short and very fair."

In spite of imposture thoroughly transparent, Oates persisted with unparalleled audacity, as he knew well the temper of
the nation. The name of " Jesuit" was to the Puritans and
to the majority of Protestants as a red rag to a bull. The
scripture was indeed verified in England, declaring that "the
hour cometh that whosoever killeth you will think that he doth
a service to God". Fanaticism, supported by calumny and
ignorance, would not hear reason, pushed aside justice, and
cared not for facts. All the private papers and correspondence

of the Jesuits were seized, but there was nothing whatsoever found upon which the slightest suspicion could rest except a few words of hope for the progress of Catholicism in England. At this crisis Sir Edmund Godfrey, the magistrate before whom Oates had made his first deposition, died. Two surgeons declared that they had found marks of violence upon his body, and then it was taken as an incontrovertible fact that the Jesuits had killed him. He was their friend, but this only aggravated their guilt, as the fanatics immediately exclaimed, " Behold of what the Jesuits are capable ! If they thus treat their friends, what will they not do to their enemies ? Their plot is discovered. They desire to poison or massacre all Protestants to the last man." The Parliament of England joined in the hue and cry, beseeching the King to guard against the dagger or the poison of the Jesuits, and in response to an offer made by Lord Shaftesbury of £500 for the discoverer of the murderer of Godfrey, a man named Bedloe claimed the reward, declared that Lord Belasyse was the instigator of the crime, and asserted that it had been committed by Jesuits in the courtyard of the residence of the Queen at Somerset House. When asked at what time the deed was committed Bedloe named a precise hour, but it transpired that at that exact time the King had been in Somerset House, with a sentinel at each entrance and a guard in the courtyard, when the murder was said to have been committed. Nothing daunted, however, by this failure, Titus Oates himself came forward and revealed a plot of the most absurd character. He said that the Pope had declared himself sovereign of Great Britain, and assigned the Government of it to Father Oliva,—General of the Society of Jesus. Lord Arundel, the Earl of Powis, Lord Belasyse, Lord Petre, Lord Talbot, and the Viscount Stafford were appointed to

hold high offices. These innocent noblemen were immediately imprisoned in the Tower. So monstrously absurd was the
entire fabrication that it really did not deceive the members of
the Government. As a proof of this we find the Protestant
Bishop Burnet saying to the arch protector of conspirators, Lord
Shattesbury, "My lord, do you not perceive that you can expect
but cut-throats for witnesses?" to which the reply was, "And
you, doctor, do you not see that the more absurd our conspiracy
is, the more will the people thirsting for the marvellous
be credulous?" This was exactly the case. Nothing was
too preposterous for a multitude whose minds had been
thoroughly poisoned by calumny. These truly infernal machinations caused six innocent men to be put to death because
they were Jesuits. These martyrs for the faith, who died
gloriously on an English scaffold, were Fathers Whitbread,
Ireland, Fenwick, Waring, Gavin, and Turner. Father
Claude de la Colombiere, chaplain of the Duchess of York,
being a French subject, was only banished from English territory. Fox in his history of the early part of the reign of
James II., says that, " In this affair witnesses so contemp-
tible that their evidence would not have been admissible
in the most insignificant cause, made statements so improb-
able or rather so impossible, that if they had even been
attested by Cato himself they could not be believed. It was
nevertheless on these depositions alone that a large number
of innocent persons were condemned to death and executed,
and several peers imprisoned. The accusers, prosecutors,
attorney-generals, pushed their accusations with all possible
fury, the juries naturally partook of the frenzy which animated the nation, and the judges themselves whose duty it
was to exhort against such impressions most scandalously
did all that they could to confirm prejudices and to imflame

passions." At the same time that the vaunted guarantee of English liberty, the *Habeas Corpus* Act, was being enacted, the inveterate thirst for the blood of innocent men induced this infamous course of tyranny. The King, the Clergy, the Parliament, the magistrates all knew that the plot of Titus Oates was a mere fabrication, but they so hated the Jesuits without cause that they put them to death without justice.

In France the Order of Jesus had to suffer very much, although in that country persecution took entirely a different form from that which it assumed in England. The Jesuits were hated by lax and irregular Catholics as well as by all coteries, such as those of the Jansenists, which were opposed to the Pope. From an early period they were marked out as men who stood aloof from political contests ; and when in 1588 even the priests and religious in Paris had declared against Henry IV. the fathers of the order scrupulously held aloof, and in this way incurred the bitter hatred of the League. The King abjured Calvinism in the Church of St Denis on the 25th July, 1593, and it was the Jesuit, Cardinal Tolet, who succeeded with difficulty in removing the ban of excommunication. So exasperated had the opposite political faction become that we find them petitioning the Parliament "to direct that this sect (the Jesuits) may be exterminated not only from the University, but also from the kingdom of France"; and a Calvinist named Bungars, writing from Paris, says : "We are engaged here in expelling the Jesuits. The University, the curates, and the entire city have united against these pests of society."

On the 27th December, 1594, John Chastel attempted to assassinate Henry IV., but only wounded him slightly. When examined the prisoner incidentally stated that he had studied philosophy under the Jesuits. This was enough for the frantic enemies of the order, who immediately accused the Society of having placed the poniard in the hands of the assassin. In vain Chastel declared until the last moments of his life, that the Jesuits had never in the slightest degree contributed to his crime by their advice or teaching. The college of the order at Clermont was searched and there were found some manuscripts and writings against Henry III. and opposed to the dignity of kings, but Hurault Chiverny, the Chancellor of France, tells us that probably these were placed there by their enemies. With cruelty and extraordinary injustice Parliament caused the Jesuits to be dragged to the conciergerie prison, the fathers at Clermont were also seized, and all members of the Society were without trial ordered to leave Paris within three days, and the kingdom within fifteen days, under the threat that if found within the realm after that period they would be put to death. But this was not enough. Father Guignard was seized and cruelly tortured. He had nothing to reveal and it was impossible for him to confess crimes of which he was perfectly innocent. The inveterate hatred of Calvinism was too powerful, and this Confessor of the Faith was ordered to be ignominiously hanged on the Place de Greve, and his body burned to ashes. L'Estaile in his *Memoirs of Henry IV.* (tome iii., p. 109) tells us that Father Guignard, having been conducted to the scaffold, prayed for the king and exhorted the people to reverence and obey him. He asked them also to pray for the Jesuits and not to lightly believe false reports charging them with being assassins of kings. The last words and calm holy death of this martyr produced a great effect, but the work of vengeance still went on. The Jesuits were banished, their property was confiscated, and their reputation grossly calumniated. An inscription on a

8

pyramid erected in a prominent part of Paris, after referring to the arrest of Chastel, thus alludes to the martyred father and to the Order of Jesus to which he belonged :—

"A detestable parricide, imbued with the pestilential heresy of this pernicious sect, which lately covering the most abominable crimes under the veil of piety, publicly teaching that kings, the anointed of the Lord, should be killed, has endeavoured to assassinate Henry IV.".

History repeats itself. This falsehood is very similar in character to that inscribed on the monument in London stating that the city had been set on fire by the Catholics.*

The great library of the Jesuits in Paris was pillaged, and under a specious pretence of distributing the confiscated property of the order for pious uses, pensions were secured to the principal Calvinists, while several leading ministers and others were installed in their house at Clermont. The order calmly and silently submitted to insults, to calumny, to persecution. Cretineau Joly tells us (tome ii., p. 378), that some of the persecuted Fathers died in dungeons, but that the most of them were forced to leave France. They were victims to the vengeance of the enemies of the Church. In order to give Henry IV. time to calm men's minds, the Jesuits endured without recrimination the outrages of the Calvinists, and of the new leaguers who had allied themselves to heresy. They preserved the dignity of silence.

Henry IV. was the protector and friend of the Jesuits. He admired the spirit and constitution of the Society, and joined his entreaties to those of other sovereigns for the canonisation of its founder. His death was a loss of serious

---

* See Pope, *The Monument :*
          "Like a tall bully lifts its head and lies ".

consequence, and the blow which Ravaillac struck at the King was also aimed at religion. Incredible although it seems, nevertheless it is a fact that the Jesuits were charged with this murder. The evidence is as preposterous as the charge. Six months before the deed was committed Ravaillac had been seen talking in public with Father Aubigny in the Church of the professed house. A book by Father Mariana which taught that the assassination of tyrants was permissible had been condemned by the Society, but the prejudice of the Parliament and University was so great that they completely ignored this fact, and attributed to the order teaching which it had positively condemned. The Lutherans and Calvinists basely disseminated this most atrocious and most absurd calumny, and at last the Bishop of Paris deemed it just to declare publicly that as " Since the cruel parricide committed on the person of the deceased King several reports have been spread in this city of Paris to the great prejudice of the Jesuit Fathers, we, desirous of preserving the honour and reputation of that order, having fully seen that such reports have originated only in ill will, founded on animosity against the said Fathers, do by these presents declare to all those whom it may concern, that the said reports are frauds and calumnies, maliciously invented against them, to the detriment of the Roman Catholic and Apostolic religion ; and not only that the said Fathers are free from such blame, but, moreover, that their order is, by its doctrine, as well as by its edifying life, of the greatest service to the Church of God and to this State ".

Among the curiosities of history are to be ranked the extraordinarily irrational and unfounded calumnies which from time to time urged on the enemies of the Catholic Church to the hatred and persecution of its most devoted

and most efficient supporters—the members of the Society
of Jesus.   In no order has the words of our Saviour respecting the undeserved persecution which awaited his
followers been more amply fulfilled.   In spite of the rage
and hatred of their enemies the Jesuits were allowed to live
in France, as they were the most learned and efficient instructors of youth in Europe.   The clergy, princes, and
nobility saw this clearly, and used their powerful influence
to retain them.   The Prince de Condé abjured Calvinism,
and declared in favour of the Jesuits.   Father Coton was
confessor to the young king.   Father John de Sufferin was
appointed confessor to the Queen Regent, and Father Mar-
guestand to the Princess Elizabeth.   The Duke of Longue-
ville favoured them in Picardy, the Cardinal (Joyeuse)
Archbishop of Rouen markedly showed his confidence in
them, eleven of the principal colleges of the Quartier Latin
were united to those of the Jesuits, and the University
became almost deserted.

Under the regime of Cardinal Richelieu, the enemies of
the order in France obtained an opportunity of displaying
their animosity.   Father Santarelli had published in Latin
at Rome a work in which the rights of the Holy See as
regards princes were defended in the most complete manner.
The book was written in defence of liberty, so disast-
rously assailed in France and other kingdoms of Europe.   It
gave offence, of course, to all the courtiers and time-servers
of the period, and was seized upon as a handle by the
enemies of the Society.   It mattered nothing that this work
had been published in Italy as an exposition of views held
in that country, and in no way proceeding from the Fathers
of the order in France.   The Attorney-General took it upon
himself publicly to assail innocent men, and thus find favour

with the authorities. On the 6th of March, 1626, in presence of the King and Parliament he commenced a harangue endeavouring to show the evil of handing over youth to be instructed in the principles held by Jesuits, but he never finished his discourse. He had scarcely concluded the exordium when he fell dead, from a stroke of apoplexy. Shortly afterwards, however, another man was found to take his place. The Provincial and the Superiors of the Jesuits were summoned before the bar of the Parliament. Fathers Coton, Filleau, Brossold, and Armand were ordered to sign four articles, when the first named declared : " We are ready to sign that which the Society of the Sorbonne and the assembly of the clergy themselves sign ". This reply checkmated the enemies of the Society, but Father Coton, who was in weak health, was hurried to death by persecution, and passed away to his reward a few days after the occurrence mentioned. When dying, he raised his feeble hands to Heaven, and this faithful and patriotic soul cried out, " Must I then die like a criminal, guilty of high treason, and as a disturber of the public peace, after having served two kings of France with so much fidelity during thirty years?" Father Coton had died for his order, the sacrifice was accepted, and the storm ceased.

The second half of the seventeenth century was a period in which the labours of the Society were peculiarly fruitful. In France, conversions were numerous and important. The Count de la Suze and the Marquis de Beauvais abjured Calvinism at the parent house in Paris; Louis de Croy at Usez ; the Countess de Montpinçon at Alençon ; all the La Claye family at Meaux. The tide had turned against Protestantism, and these were among the first fruits of a great harvest. At the same period Count Dunois entered

the novitiate of the Society, and Father Vincent Huby
founded in Brittany the first houses of retreat which subsequently became so numerous throughout Europe and in
South America.

In France Jansenism raised its head, and as its chief
object was to attack the lawful authority of the head of the
Church, it naturally succeeded in at once securing the
favour of all infidels and heretics. The Jesuit Fathers in
Paris endeavoured with conciliatory kindness to heal the
breach, but in vain. The Jansenists were continually
animated by bitter hatred of an order which has always
been to the Church militant what the household troops are
to a sovereign. They honoured the Jesuits by identifying
them with the Catholic doctrine respecting the Pope, and
manifested their opposition to both by a course of powerful
opposition to constituted authority. The Solitaires of Port
Royal declared that they would submit to the Holy See,
and an opportunity came to test this statement. By a Bull,
dated 31st May, 1653, Pope Innocent X. decided against
Jansenism and that several of the opinions held by this sect
were heretical. The Jansenist deputies who had been sent
to Rome endeavoured to ruin the Jesuits in the estimation
of the Pope and of the Sacred College. In France, the
supporters of Port Royal became enthusiasts in favour of
the party of the Fronde and of Cardinal de Retz, and thus
gained immense political power. They insidiously declared
that they joined with the Church in opposing what the Bull
declared heretical, but that the obnoxious propositions condemned could not be attributed to the doctrines of Jansenius.
They stated that the Jesuits alone maintained that they
were found there. So far did the Archbishop of Sens
proceed that on the 26th of January, 1653, he took the

extreme step of excommunicating the Fathers of the Jesuit College in his diocese. France became divided into factions —Jansenist and Molinist. The Fronde declared for the former, and the Mazarin party was in favour of the Jesuits. In the midst of this dreadful turmoil, the members of the Society tranquilly did their duty, and Father Bagot was able in Paris to collect together a number of young men with religious vocations, who felt called to the apostleship of the faith in distant countries. This was the origin of one of the most illustrious and useful organisations in the world—the society of foreign missions.

The Church and all societies of the Church suffer severely from absolute monarchy. Liberty forms an atmosphere of health for religion, but tyranny whether of the mob or of the sovereign is always most destructive. Louis XIV. was undoubtedly a ruler whose will was law, and his arbitrary commands extremely fettered the operations of the Society. Changes which struck at discipline were imperatively ordered, and on the 26th of April, 1688, the king of France went so far as to order Father Paul Fontaine, Assistant of France, to return to his kingdom with the other French Fathers then in Rome. On the 11th of October following, Louis XIV. commanded those Jesuits who were his subjects not to correspond with their General. From this dictatorial sovereign the greatest difficulties were experienced. He even went so far as to recommend that five provinces should be governed irrespective of the General. To this it was replied "that the misunderstanding now existing between the King of France and the General of the Society will terminate at latest on the death of one or the other, and I have great hopes that it will end sooner. It would not be thus were the authority of the General attacked ;

its loss would be irreparable." The monarch of France was so unused to the least opposition that his astonishment was even greater than his chagrin; but it is to be recorded in his favour that he finally submitted.

One of the charges most frequently brought against the Society is that of desiring to acquire political power, and it is certainly one of the most ill-founded. Nothing is more destructive to evangelisation and teaching than the strife of parties, and therefore the Jesuits have always most sedulously held aloof as far as it was in their power. When Joseph I., Emperor of Germany, compelled his confessor, a Jesuit, to take an active part in State affairs, the General (Father Thyrsus Gonzales de Santalla) severely censured the Father and summoned him to Rome. When the order was made imperative, and the Pope's Nuncio urged the necessity of obedience, the Emperor replied—"Tell the Father-General that if, contrary to my wish, my confessor must go to Rome, he shall not go alone ; for all the Jesuits in my States shall accompany him, and be prohibited returning". As the interests of religion in a Protestant country would have been seriously jeopardised by the withdrawal of a number of Priests, the General was very unjustly compelled to yield. James II. of England desired to raise his Jesuit confessor to the Episcopate; and upon the Pope objecting, the King took umbrage and demanded a Cardinal's hat for him. In this matter James was obliged to yield to the opposition of autho- rity, but he was sufficiently unwise to compel Father Petre to enter the Privy Council. The Father-General was gravely displeased at one of the order being thus forced into the political arena, but his protests were in vain. The enemies of the order and of religion obtained a handle which they used to the utmost. It was gravely alleged that the

Society reigned under the name of James, and that a dreadful slaughter of Protestants was therefore imminent. This was one of the principal pretexts for depriving the Stuarts of the crown, and a device to which William of Orange and the family which produced "the four Georges" owed much of their success.

That the attitude of the Jesuits in opposition to Jansenism was perfectly accurate there can be no question, as by the celebrated Bull "*unigenitus,*" issued at Rome on the 8th of September, 1713, the Holy See condemned the *Reflexions Morales* as containing several heresies, and among others · all those of Jansenius. Previously, in 1707, the Nuns of Port Royal had been severely censured and prohibited from approaching the Sacraments. In the year following Clement XI. suppressed their Convent by a Bull in which their establishment was designated as "the hotbed of heresy". One of the great figures of the time was Pere la Chaise, the Jesuit confessor of Louis XIV. for more than thirty years, whose piety, patience, and zeal for religion were most edifying. Pere Letellier, S.J., was his successor. When he appeared before the King, His Majesty inquired if he were a relative of the Chancellor, Michael Letellier. "I, sire," was the reply, "a relative of the Letelliers! Nothing of the sort. I am a poor peasant, the son of a farmer of La Basse Normandie." The Christians of the time seemed to forget that our Saviour was on earth the reputed son of a carpenter. Pride, which helped to cause the French revolution, permeated the court and nobility, so we cannot be surprised to learn that the humble birth of the Jesuit Father caused him to be treated with hostility and contempt. St. Simon says that Father Letellier was "from the dregs of the people, and made no secret of it". In France the entire order was for many years persecuted and harassed because of their opposition to heresy in the form of Jansenism, and to pride and sensuality in connection with the Court and the nobility. King Louis XIV. chose his confessors from the Society, and appreciated its value; but no sooner was he succeeded by the infamous Duke of Orleans, notorious for his public and degrading vices, than the Jansenists were taken into favour and Father Letellier banished.

In 1720 the plague broke out at Marseilles. It was in such a field that the Society of Jesus ever showed its single-hearted devotion and undaunted bravery. The Bishop of Marseilles had belonged to the order and knew what could be expected from its members. He was not disappointed. While one thousand victims were carried off in a day, and those of the municipal officers who had not fled were seized by the dreadful disease, all the Jesuits remained at their posts and were indefatigable in their attendance on the plague-stricken. Father Mellery helped to administer the affairs of the city. Eighteen of the Fathers fell victims of charity. One alone survived—Father John Peter Levert— who had nursed plague-stricken people in the missions of the East, and now at the age of eighty, with untiring zeal, devoted himself to a renewal of these labours. But he had to succumb to his exertions, and shortly after the cessation of the plague died in the arms of the Bishop with whom he had so gloriously laboured. Thirty-eight Jesuits fell victims of charity in Marseilles, Aix, Arles, Avignon, and Toulon.

CHAPTER VI.

*Jansenism and infidelity in France. The Jesuits suppressed
in France, Spain, and Portugal. Fathers Nethard and
Daubenton. Infidel conspiracy against the Society.
King of Spain deceived by forgeries. Persecutions in
Spain, Portugal, Italy, and South America. The
Emperor Nicholas I. of Paraguay. Cruel Persecu-
tions of De Pombal.*

JANSENISTS, Protestants, and Infidels united together
in France to oppose the Jesuits. On one side
were the various assailants of the Church of Christ,
and on the other her staunch and constant defenders.
The Pope declared against Jansenism, but that only increased the rage of the enemies of Catholicism. Gross and
scandalous licentiousness under the Regency, and during
the reign of Louis XV., formed a hotbed, which produced
infidelism and subsequent revolution. The Protestant historian, Ranke, tells us (tome iii., p. 344 *et seq.*) that a party
was formed which founded its hatred of all religion on a
system which destroyed all idea of a God and all the
essential principles of authority and society. Notwithstand-
ing the apparent diversity of opinions between Jansenists,
Protestants, and Atheists, he tells us that all these parties
were united against the Church and the Jesuits. Then, as
now, society had only one firm support—Catholicism ; and
we see in France during many years preceding the time of

Danton and Robespierre the agencies of evil sapping the supports of order and trying to destroy the pillars which upheld it. Like another Samson, the strong powers of infidelism ended by burying both themselves and their countrymen in the ruin of the edifice they succeeded in pulling down. Hatred and opposition to the Society showed itself in calumnies and persecution whenever these were possible. At one time it was an absurd statement in Toulon (1731) that the Jesuits had caused a holy young woman to be possessed by an evil spirit. Pamphlets and songs were issued, and the absurd scandal did not cease until a parliamentary decree proclaiming the innocence of the Father who had been maligned was promulgated. At another time (1746) immense sums were said to have been extorted from a widow, and this was not finally disposed of until a dying man juridcally declared before competent witnesses that he had falsely sworn to the truth of this statement.* It would be impossible to detail within reasonable limits all the cases in which the most gross calumnies against the Jesuits have been utterly disproved. The advice of Calvin to his followers has been most carefully attended to : " Calumniate, calumniate, something will always remain ".

The Protestant historian, Ranke, points out one of the principal causes of the temporary suppression of the order. He tells us that Reforming Ministers were placed at the

* The man was a Fleming named Jusse Dervosen, and he made his dying deposition at the Hotel Dieu in Paris in 1746. The case of Father de Lavalette gave an occasion for calumniating the order in respect to financial matters ; but the Father was honest although imprudent, and his entering into commercial transactions was quite condemned by the Father-General.

helm in almost all the Catholic states—in France, Choiseul; in Spain, Wall and Squillace; in Naples, Tanucci; in Portugal, Carvalho—all men who had made it the main thought and object of their life to limit the pretensions of the Church. In them the ecclesiastical opposition acquired representatives and champions; their individual position rested upon it; and open war was the more inevitable, since they found the Jesuits constantly labouring to obstruct their designs by personal counteractions and by personal influence over the highest classes of society. France was the most infidel country, and it was there that the enemies of religion first triumphed over the Jesuits. On the 1st of April, 1762, the Jesuit colleges were closed by order of the Parliament of Paris; and simultaneously over the length and breadth of the land pamphlets were distributed charging the order with preposterous crimes. These charges, like overdoses of poison, really neutralised themselves, but nevertheless Calvin was right. If plenty of mud be thrown some of it may stick. The Jesuits were not only guilty of sorcery, blasphemy, idolatry, and magic, but they were even charged with favouring religious heresies, sects, and schisms. Nothing was proved, for the excellent reason that nothing could be proved; but abuse was adopted instead of argument, and mere calumny in lieu of evidence. All the freethinkers united in praising the Parliament for prosecuting the Jesuit Fathers. It is noticeable that those people who have talked loudest about liberty of conscience have generally been those to respect it the least. The members of the Parliament were flattered by the approval of men of rank and of literary ability. The mandatory letters of bishops were publicly burnt, and the Pope's briefs favouring the Society of Jesus were suppressed. The clergy by petition earnestly asked for the preservation of the order, but the infidels were too strong. D'Alambert, writing to Voltaire, says of the members of the Parliament : "They serve reason without suspecting it ; they are the high executioners for philosophy (free thinking), whose orders they take without knowing it". The clergy of France in vain pointed out that it was contrary to the dictates of justice, against the rules of the Church, and in opposition to the civil law to destroy an entire Society without cause. The licentious Louis XV. was ruled by mistresses, and left the affairs of State to Choiseul, his Prime Minister. The farce of getting the Attorney-General's report on the Order of Jesus was adopted, and his opinion was accepted as superior to that of the clergy, the Sovereign Pontiffs, and the Council of Trent. In the midst of national decadence and corruption it is refreshing to perceive that the Courts of Flanders, Artois, Alsace, and Besançon distinguished themselves by declaring in favour of justice and truth. They distinctly refused to admit that the Jesuits were the enemies of religion and the State, while the magistracy of Lorraine announced that it considered the Jesuits to be "the most faithful subjects of the King of France and the best guarantees of the morals of the people". All was in vain. The sluice-gates of the revolution were made ready for opening ; infidelism triumphed ; and on the 6th of August, 1762, the Parliament of Paris issued a decree depriving the Jesuits, not merely of their churches, colleges, and homes, but even of their furniture and libraries. A reformation like that of John Knox in Scotland was effected—a reformation founded upon robbery and spoliation. The weak Louis XV. himself declared: "I am not cordially in favour of the Jesuits; but they have been always detested by every heresy". The French episcopacy, headed by the venerable and saintly Archbishop of Paris, urged his Majesty in vain to stop this act of iniquity; and on the 7th of January, 1765, Pope Clement XIII., in the Bull *Apostolicum*, condemned the expulsion, and termed it a serious injury inflicted on the Church and the Holy See.

Spain and Portugal comprised good ground, which produced a hundred-fold so far as the Society was concerned. After the defeat of the Moors the nation rose, as if under a new baptism, to a healthy and vigorous Christian life. The Viceroy of Catalonia, Duke of Gandia, became famous as St. Francis Borgia, one of the most devoted Generals of the order. Fathers Lefevre and Araoz preached with the utmost success. Numerous hospitals and educational establishments' were founded, and great success attended the labours of the Fathers. The College of Coimbra became a very flourishing institution, and it was here that men from many of the most noble families entered the order. Among these were Melchior Nunez, Noguerra, Louis de Grana, Carnero, Gonsalvo Silveira, and Rodrigue de Menezes. In the year 1546 there were colleges in the towns of Gandia, Barcelona, Valencia, and Alcala. At Salamanca the Dominican monk Melchior Cano was encountered, who styled the Fathers of the Society precursors of Anti-Christ ! The General of the Dominicans intervened ; and, remembering how grevously his own order had been caluminated, issued an official order, in which he vindicates the Society of Jesus. " We order each one of you by these presents, with the authority with which we are charged, by virtue of the Holy Spirit and of holy obedience, and under penalties which we can choose, not to have the audacity in any way to calumniate the Society of Jesus or its constitutions, approved of by the Holy See, or to speak of its members unfavourably. On the contrary, we desire you to aid this order and its priests, as your companions in arms, and to protect and to defend them against their adversaries."

In 1566 there were in Spain four Provincials—James Carillo for Castile, Gonzales Gonzalve for Toledo, James d'Avellanada for Andalusia, and Alphonsus Roman for Arragon. Not only were there numerous colleges and schools for Christians, but in Cadiz the religious instruction of the Moors bore immense fruit, and at Grenada numerous conversions were made. Father Balthazar Alvares was the Director who conducted the great St. Teresa in the ways of perfection, while St. Francis Borgia, as the General of the order, shone forth a most noble example of sanctity and devotion. This century was one in which the plague devastated Europe, and in the cities stricken by this awful calamity the devotion of the Fathers of the order was heroic and memorable. In Toledo (1571) Father John Martinez was found dead among the corpses, where he had been stretched to hear the confessions of the dying. The Jesuits could not but observe the evil effects to national character which arose from the brutal but exceedingly popular bull-fights, which formed one of the favourite national spectacles. Pius V. shared the sentiments of the Jesuit Fathers; and in a pontifical decree, addressed to the inhabitants of Cordova, prohibited bull-fights, and characterised them as spectacles which should fill Christians with horror. The Cordovans had the good sense and the humanity to renounce these cruel sports.

In the latter half of the sixteenth century, colleges were founded in Spain at Soria, Oviedo, Ferrol, and Pampeluna. Houses of the order were established in Valencia and

Seville. The land of St. Teresa and of Ignatius Loyola could not but be favourable for the order; nevertheless it was by ecclesiastics in Spain that many charges were made against the nature and character of the Society. By order of the General (Everard Mercurian) these were triumphantly answered by Father Ribadeneira,* who had been the friend both of Loyola and of Laynès. During the reign of Philip, who ruled over the united kingdoms of Spain and Portugal, the Jesuits acquired immense powers of usefulness. Their churches, colleges, and schools were numerous and successful. Although that monarch was dignified with the title of "Catholic King," and undoubtedly was in many respects worthy of the great honour, he evidently loved the exercise of power, and rather encouraged attacks upon the Jesuits, so that the order might be as much as possible at his mercy. He wished both to glorify and to rule the order, but the Society could not and would not sacrifice its independence. Certain Spanish Fathers gave great trouble in desiring to effect changes in the Constitutions of the Society, as their efforts were countenanced and assisted by the Spanish Inquisition and the Government. The General (Aquaviva), although greatly tried and harassed, acted so as to secure the approval of the Holy Father, and the protection of his order from innovations and dangerous changes.

It was at the end of the year 1617, and in the midst of the greatest public testimonies of respect, that the body of St. Francis Borgia was translated from Rome to Madrid. All Spain implored the Holy See to declare him a saint whose life had so honoured humanity, and whose virtues

* The author of the very valuable *Lives of the Saints,* of which there is an English translation published last century.

were a title of glory to the Society he loved so much. Philip III. died in 1621, and in his last moments sent for Father Jerome de Florentia, who has been styled the Bourdalaue of Spain, to console him. His successor, Philip IV., greatly loved and protected the Society. Numerous colleges were founded for all classes. In the words of Cretineau Joly : " The plan of the Fathers was not to concentrate education among the privileged orders. They called the children of the poor and the heirs of noble houses to enjoy in common the benefits of instruction. They established Christian equality; they made it reign over youth in order to engrave its principles on the heart of man." The Society performed wonderful educational and evangelical works throughout the entire peninsula. As the enemies of the Catholic Church always seize with extraordinary avidity upon any event which can be supposed to throw discredit upon the Jesuits, we cannot be surprised to read in the French *Encyclopædia*—article "Jesuits"—that "In 1646 the Fathers at Seville became bankrupt, which precipitated many families into misery". The simple fact is that the college at Seville had as temporal administrator a coadjutor brother, who, in order to procure means for the establishment, entered into commercial speculations which were unfortunate. His superiors were unaware of his conduct, and he himself declared that all creditors would be satisfied, and kept his word. Nevertheless he was expelled from the Society, and specially bore witness to the fact that he alone, and not the order, should bear any blame connected with his conduct.

Towards the middle of the seventeenth century an agitation arose throughout Portugal in favour of declaring that country independent of Spain, and placing it under the rule of the

Duke of Braganza. Naturally several Portuguese Fathers sympathised with the patriotic aspirations of their country-men; but the Provincial, in accordance with the uniform custom of the order, sternly repressed all political manifes-tations. The laws of the general congregations are most clear on this subject; and at all times and in all places all members of the Society are interdicted from encouraging sedition, directly or indirectly, by public or by tacit appro-bation. The separation of Portugal and Spain became an accomplished fact, and the Duke of Braganza sat upon the throne in Lisbon. The Jesuits first arrived in Portugal when commercial success, riches, great theatres, luxury, and enervating vice had virtually ruined the Portuguese. The nation began to decline from these causes, and because of the persistent hostility of its more powerful neighbour, Spain. Decadence gradual but most certain took place; and although this was delayed to some extent by the Jesuits, it was im-possible for them to prevent it. The same teaching power which did so much for France, for Catholic Germany, and for Poland, did not succeed, because it could not succeed in Portugal. A person of this time referred to in the *Bibliotheca Lusitana* as one of the most illustrious men which Portugal ever produced, was Father Antony Vieira, theologian, poet, orator, philosopher and historian. He was distinguished as much for his energy and force of character as for his mental gifts. He was sent as ambassador to Paris, to Rome, and to Holland. In the last named country he triumphed in a public discussion at Amsterdam over the famous Rabbi Manasses-Ben-Israel. This great man did his best to reform the Portuguese nation, and his efforts were most nobly seconded by other Fathers. The Society supplied confessors to the kings of Portugal as well as to the monarchs

of Spain, and in the former kingdom this circumstance re-
sulted in disastrous feelings of jealousy and hatred. "They
have hated me without a cause."

In Spain the weakness and imbecility of the monarchs
were fatal to the progress and prosperity of the kingdom.
Father Nithard, the confessor of Mary Anne of Austria,
wife of Philip IV., had been a famous professor of moral
philosophy at the university of Gratz, and had directed the
studies of the children of the Emperor Ferdinand III. This
great scholar and able administrator had reached the ripe
age of sixty, when in Spain he was called upon by Pope
Alexander III. to perform the duties of Inquisitor-General
and Councillor of State. He belonged to a society which
detested luxury, idleness, and all the vices which were then
fast sapping the foundations of the great Spanish monarchy.
The wealth of the Indies was squandered in follies, while
industry and manufactures languished. Father Nithard was
a type of those statesmen who might have saved the country,
if intrigue had not been too strong. Don John of Austria
made himself his enemy, and Father Nithard was found guilty
on vague accusations and without a trial. As the Protestant
historian Coxe says* :—" Father Nithard has reduced to their
just proportions the vague and non-proved accusations of
Don Juan, in other respects an estimable prince, nevertheless ambitious and impulsive, and who in this affair used
means which both honour and conscience condemn". The
same author adds that Father Nithard refused to accept the
honours and emoluments which the Government of Spain
designed to bestow upon him. "He preferred," to employ
his own expression, "to quit Spain as he had come into it—

* *Spain under the Kings of the House of Bourbon*, vol. i, introd. p. 37.

a poor priest." He was sent as ambassador from Spain to the Holy See, and in 1673 received the Cardinal's hat from Pope Clement X.

Father Daubenton became through the force of circumstances and his own ability one of the statesmen of Spain. He was sent there by Louis XIV. as confessor to the young King, Philip V., and endeavoured to prevent abuses. Father Robinet succeeded him, and is described as a man of great enlightenment and virtue, full of patriotic zeal for his native country, France, and for his adopted country, Spain. A just and noble action caused him to retire from a country for whose "interests and those of religion he unceasingly laboured". He had recommended the King to fill worthily the Archiepiscopal See of Toledo which had become vacant, by appointing to it a most excellent Spanish Bishop in every way suited for the office. The King consented, but so enraged was the party in the State, who wished to nominate a foreigner of their own choice, that the weak monarch gave way and permitted Father Robinet, his capable, honourable councillor, to retire to the house of the Jesuits at Strasburg. Father Daubenton was recalled by the King, and became his confessor. At this time the wild schemes and mad projects of the Prime Minister (Alberoni) threatened to plunge Europe into war; but the Jesuit confessor, by his sound advice, was fortunately able to avert these terrible evils and to save the civilised world from that destruction which is frequently the consequence of inordinate ambition.

On the 26th of March, 1766, a popular outbreak took place at Madrid, which was quickly and thoroughly appeased by the influence of the Jesuit priests of the city, whom the people knew and loved. The danger at one time seemed so great that the King, Charles III., fled from his capital. He felt humiliated when he found himself enabled to return, not by means of the bayonets of soldiers, but by the good offices of monks. This imbecile monarch was easily made a tool by the enemies of the Society, who represented to him that the Jesuits had caused the outbreak in order to gain fame and authority by repressing it. This absurdity is no greater than most of the other calumnies which have been periodically used against the order. The Marquis de Choiseul and all the infidels, or self-styled philosophers of Europe, saw in the Jesuits the strongest defenders of religion, and were accordingly determined to destroy the Society. No opportunity, was neglected. The Protestant historian Coxe* tells us that in 1764, "The French minister proposed to complete the destruction of the Jesuits in other countries. He endeavoured above everything to obtain their complete banishment from Spanish territory. To this end Choiseul did not spare any effort or any intrigue for the purpose of spreading alarm concerning their principles and their character. He attributed to them all the faults which could possibly be used against the order. He had not the least scruple in circulating forged letters in the name of their General and other superiors, and to spread odious calumnies against members of the Society. . . . Above all things rumours were circulated relative to their supposed plots and conspiracies against the Spanish Government. To give a semblance of truth to the accusation, a letter was fabricated, which purported to be written by the General of the order at Rome, and addressed to the Provincial in Spain. This letter ordered him to stir up insurrections. It had been sent in such a way as to be intercepted.† Stories were circulated about

---

* *Spain under the House of Bourbon.*

† This was exactly one of the plans adopted by Titus Oates *in re* Papist Plot in England.

the immense riches and estates of the fathers. . . . The principal cause of their expulsion (from Spain) was the success of the means employed to make the King believe that it was by their intrigues that the outbreak at Madrid had been excited, and that they were still forming new machinations against both his family and his person. Influenced by these opinions, Charles became their implacable enemy; he became eager to follow the example of the French Government in driving from his dominions a Society which seemed to him to be so dangerous." The Protestant historian Leopold Ranke agrees with Coxe; Christopher De Murr and Sismondi are of the same opinion, and Schœll, another Protestant, declares: "Since in 1764 * the Duke of Choiseul had expelled the Jesuits from France, he persecuted that order also in Spain. All means were employed to make the order an object of terror to the King, and success was at last obtained by means of an atrocious calumny. They placed under the King's eyes a pretended letter of Père Ricci, General of the Jesuits, which the Duke of Choiseul is accused of having fabricated; a letter in which the General was made to announce to his correspondent that he had succeeded in collecting documents which incontestably proved that Charles III. was the offspring of adultery. This absurd invention made such an impression on the King that it determined him to expel the Jesuits." The English historian Adam in his *History of Spain* adopts the same view, and in this way we are afforded a plain and natural explanation of the manner in which a religious and Catholic but weak monarch was induced suddenly to become the bitter enemy of an order which he had previously loved and protected. It is to cruel

---

* *Cours d'Histoire des Etats Europeans*, tome xxxix., p. 163.

calumnies proceeding from the malignant hatred of infidels and heretics that we must trace the extraordinary persecutions of the Jesuits. In most European countries preposterous and incorrect ideas are still entertained of the nature and objects of the Society. Mere general statements, quite unaccompanied by the slightest proof, are relied on; and an entire order, devoted to self-abnegation, religion, and works of mercy, is condemned without evidence, without reason, and without justice.

The Government of Ferdinand VII. publicly announced that the Society of Jesus was for ever banished by virtue of a measure obtained from Charles III. by the most unscrupulous and iniquitous means. This banishment was serious, as it embraced not only Spain but the Spanish possessions in the New World. In South America the Jesuits could easily have incited the people to throw off the yoke of the home country; but instead of making any effort in this direction, they submitted with meekness and patience. The traveller Page,* in his voyage to the Philippines, says: "I am not able to conclude this just eulogium of the Jesuits without remarking that in a position where the extreme attachment of the natives would, with very little encouragement, have led them into insurrection, I saw them obey the decree of their abolition with the deference due to the civil authority, and at the same time with the calmness and the firmness of truly heroic souls". Sismondi† says: "In Mexico, in Peru, in Chili, even in the Philippines, they were invested in their colleges, their papers seized, their persons arrested and banished. Their resistance in the missions, where they were adored by

* Vol. ii., p. 190.   † *Histoire des Francais*, t. xxix., p. 372.

the converts, was feared ; but, so far from resisting, they displayed resignation and humility united to truly heroic calmness and firmness." Pope Clement XIII. in vain appealed to the infatuated King of Spain in favour of the Society. His Holiness called God to witness "that the body, the institution, the spirit of the Society of Jesus are innocent; this Society is not only innocent, it is pious, useful, and holy in its object". D'Aranda in Spain, Choiseul in France, Pombal in Portugal, were members of the infidel oligarchy which at that period really dominated Europe. Without conscience or scruple they used the basest means to destroy the Jesuits, because they were " the most able and most constant defenders of religion and of the Church ". * Unjust confiscations and cruel exile were insisted upon with extreme severity. Six thousand Fathers were deported to the States of the Church in order to embarrass the Holy Father ; and in Parma one of the fiefs of the Holy See, an agent of the philosophic sect named Du Tillot, poisoned the mind of the young and weak Duke of Parma, so as to secure the banishment of the Society from this part of Italy. Tanucci performed a similar office in Naples. The Bourbon family and their infidel ministers were on one side, and the people on the other. As a proof of this fact we know that, when on the 4th of November, 1768, the fete day of Charles of Spain, that monarch went out on the balcony of his palace, in accordance with custom, to grant that favour which the public generally might demand, the masses of people cried out with one voice for the reinstatement of the Jesuits in Spain.† They were always loved as the real friends of the

---

* Pope Clement XIII., quoted by the Protestant Sismondi (*Histoire des Francais,* t. xxix.).

† See Coxe (*Spain under the Kings of the House of Bourbon,* vol. v., p. 25).

poor ; and it is the rich and powerful, not the lowly and humble, who have generally been their enemies.

The Marquis de Pombal, the greatest enemy of religion and of the Jesuits in Portugal, added the grossest ingratitude to the vices of cruelty and impiety. Through making false pretences of a desire to reform abuses, he obtained the favourable recommendation of the Confessor of the Infante; but no sooner had he obtained the reins of power than he began to flatter the pride and pander to the passions of the imbecile and careless monarch who nominally governed the realm. In 1754, King Joseph I. was induced to sign a decree declaring it high treason for any one to make an attempt on the life of the Prime Minister. The next step was to invent a conspiracy for placing Don Pedro on the throne, in which it was asserted that the Jesuits took part. There was no difficulty with rulers of the Bourbon type, such as Louis XV. of France and Charles III. of Spain, while Joseph I., who was in no way superior to these monarchs, was also deceived by forgeries and calumnies. In this case, again, we find the persecutors and haters of the order not to consist of the people nor of any honourable men among the governing classes, but of the Monarch swayed by men devoid of faith and principle who hesitated at no falsehood, meanness, or cruelty which could advance the objects they had in view. Fathers Fonseca and Bannister were apprehended and exiled, but further proceedings were arrested by the awful earthquake at Lisbon, which took place on the 1st November, 1755. This was an occasion when the Fathers consoled and encouraged the sufferers, and devoted themselves with great self-denial to the performance of sublime works of charity. The King could not help being moved, recalled the exiled Fathers, and began himself to lead a more moral and regular life. De Pombal, however, was determined to reign supreme, and soon obtained such influence as to make it evident that the Jesuits would be persecuted. An occasion soon presented itself. In South America, in spite of the earnest prayers of the missionaries, the tranquil and well-governed territory of Uruguay was seized upon, and the natives were most naturally irritated and incensed. The Jesuits were then unjustly charged with causing this discontent. A story was invented about the order desiring to enrich itself from gold mines, but it was impossible to continue this fable, as the Portuguese Government found, after anxious search, that no such mines existed. Another calumny had to be invented. It was boldly stated that the Jesuits reigned supreme in Paraguay, and that a brother coadjutor had been proclaimed Emperor of that country under the title of Nicholas I. Gold mines were said to supply metal from which coins were struck bearing the effigy of this new potentate. Incredible though it may seem, these absurdities were believed and greedily used as arguments against the order by the freethinkers and Protestants of Europe.

A proposed marriage between the Princess de Beira and the Duke of Cumberland was favoured by the Marquis de Pombal, as he saw in this alliance the means of placing a Protestant on the throne of Portugal. The Jesuits, who were the spiritual directors of the Royal family, were bound in duty to oppose this project, and thus, in an additional manner, incurred the hatred of the Prime Minister. Even friends of the detested order were removed from office, and their estates confiscated. The universities were handed over to the control of enemies of the Catholic Church—Jansenists, Protestants, and infidels—while the

imbecile King was kept isolated and completely under the
control of the iron will of his minister.   The Jesuits were
accused of conspiring against the State, and on the 19th of
September, 1757, three of the Court confessors were forcibly
carried off from the palace.   The Provincial issued orders
that all sufferings were to be borne in patience, and without
reply, while every honest mind in Portugal sympathised
with the Fathers, and felt indignant at the gross injustice
and cruelty exercised towards them.

The freethinkers of Europe, who considered it wise to
deny the existence of God, and to affirm that of the
Emperor Nicholas I. of Paraguay, were capable of any
calumny, and shrank at no injustice so long as the Jesuits
were its victims.   The enemies of the Society succeeded in
wresting a brief from Pope Benedict XIV. for the reformation of the Society, which His Holiness was careful to
explain so as to show that a mere report to the Holy See
was required.   The Portuguese Government immediately
took an undue advantage of this document.   In Brazil, the
papers, correspondence, and books of account of the Fathers
of the Society were seized, but they bore these persecutions, as they did those they were subjected to in Europe,
with fortitude and resignation.   To the unscrupulous De
Pombal revenge and the gratification of passion seemed the
paramount motives of action.   Like all other nobles of
Portugal, the great and eminent family of the Marquis of
Tavora disliked and distrusted the Prime Minister.   A proposed alliance between the son of the Marquis de Pombal and
the daughter of the Marquis de Tavora was declined.   Some
time after the King was proceeding to his palace from an
entertainment which had been given at the house of the
latter nobleman, when he was fired at.   It was immediately

reported throughout the city that the attempt at assassination had been made by the Marquis de Tavora. Shortly afterwards the nobleman and his family were seized; the male members of the family were placed in dungeons, and the ladies immured in convents. A month afterwards—on the 12th of January, 1759—the Jesuits were, without evidence or trial, declared to be assassins, and the Provincial, Father Henriquez, as well as Fathers Malagrida, Perdigano, Suarez, Juan de Mattos, Oliveira, and Costa were confined in the horrible dungeons of the State. Father Costa was subjected to cruel tortures, but no confession of guilt could be wrung from him. All the members of the Tavora family, with the exception of the daughter of the Marquis, were put to death on the scaffold. Pombal had then to go further. It had never been proved that the King was even slightly wounded; and in public opinion it was clear that Pombal, needing a pretext, had used one to revenge himself upon a family who had offended him, and to rid himself of the Jesuits, who obstructed his irreligious schemes. Forgery had been frequently and successfully used against the Society, and De Pombal found no difficulty in circulating severe and libellous satires against the King under the names of various Jesuit Fathers. A plan which succeeded in Spain also proved successful in Portugal, and the fruit of these efforts was a letter from Joseph I. to the Pope, announcing to His Holiness that he had determined to expel all the Jesuits from his States. With revolting hypocrisy, De Pombal declared that the object he had in view was to restore the order to conformity with the spirit of its founder. The means he adopted were gross injustice and cruel persecution. Fifteen hundred Jesuits were seized and imprisoned, while all their property was confiscated. From Brazil the devoted missionaries were deported in vessels so insufficiently found that they had to suffer frightful hardships. In Rome the Portuguese Ambassador, Almada, fabricated a Papal brief approving of the action of the Portuguese Government, and this was at once published as genuine. At this juncture, the Jesuits in Portugal had only to signify their approval of revolution, and wide extended insurrection would have been the result. This they refused to do. Following the example of our Saviour, they suffered injuries, insults, and persecution without murmuring, and with the resignation and fortitude of martyrs. Numbers were deported to the States of the Church, and there they were received with that profound respect which their virtues and sufferings deserved. The forged brief, which Almada had sent to Lisbon, was declared by the Roman Court to be a forgery, and was burned by the public executioner.

Two hundred and twenty-one Jesuits remained within the prisons of Portugal. Father Louis du Gad, Superior of the missions of China, residing at Macao, has left a precise and circumstantial account of the sufferings in which he took part. Twenty-four Jesuits were arrested at Macao, and placed in prison as if they were murderers or thieves. Their property was seized and sold by auction. The Archbishop of Cranganor and the Bishop of Cochin were proclaimed rebels, because they had refused to abandon the missions of Malabar. After a term of imprisonment, unaccompanied by any trial, the Macao Jesuits were kept four months on board ship on a voyage to Goa. Subsequently they had again to embark and endure dreadful sufferings and privations on a voyage of twenty-seven months. They arrived at Lisbon on the 16th of October,

1764. Several of the Fathers died on the way, and their lot was the happier, as no sooner did the survivors arrive than they were confined in dungeons. Father du Gad tells us : " These prisons in which we are incarcerated are a species of catacomb. The dungeon in which I am confined, and which I have frequently measured, is six feet eight inches long, four feet four inches in breadth, and ten feet in height, and is under a street. To dispel the obscurity of this subterraneous abode, we were accorded a lamp, by the light of which we read our Office and performed our other duties. There were no apertures for light save a vent-hole or grating, eight inches long, looking towards the street, which, however, was so covered by boards as to impede the ingress of fresh air. In each of these dungeons there was an elevation of from twelve to sixteen inches high, formed of planks. It was on this that my companions and myself deposited our scanty baggage and miserable beds. It would be difficult to believe how much we suffered in wet weather in consequence of the water which percolated through and trickled down the walls, and made everything mouldy and rotten. The space that remained for us for exercise was not more than five feet. We were enclosed by two strong doors, secured by bolts. These doors were opened twice a day, morning and evening, just long enough to pass in our food and receive back the empty dishes. The food was plain and scanty, sufficient to sustain a man in tolerable health, but totally inadequate to the restoration of the sick. Nothing could be more wretched than the condition of those who were afflicted with infirmities. . . . . Our clothing having been a hundred times repaired was soon in tatters. . . . . No matter what our sufferings were for the want of common necessaries, they were borne in pa-

tience ; but that which grieved us most of all was our being
deprived of the sacraments.   It sometimes happened that
such obstacles were thrown in the way that one of our
number died without this heavenly support.   We had
neither books nor papers, or if we occasionally procured
some, it was with the greatest difficulty.   We found seventy
other Jesuits from various parts of the world.   One of them
had already suffered a nine years' imprisonment ; fifteen had
been incarcerated for seven years ; the remainder had reached
the fifth or sixth year of their captivity.   Besides the eight
Procurators of the missions, were to be seen the Father
Provincial, a Professor of the University of Evora, and
another who had filled one of the chairs at Coimbra for
nineteen years, and subsequently became superior of various
colleges.   We had also Father Alessandra, who had been
represented in the libels as one of the three who had attempted the life of the King, and who was not aware of the
charge until he had been in prison for eight years, and then
heard it quite accidentally.   Among these heroes of patience,
some were eighty years old, some seventy, others approaching sixty, the rest being aged.   Several were afflicted with
grave infirmities—some being blind, others deaf. . . . .   In
fine, all presented such an abject appearance as to call for
the remark from even the very guards, that it was almost a
miracle that they should continue to live at all.   And yet
in the midst of so much misery, and during the space of
eight years, only twelve died, our Lord, in His goodness,
being pleased to accord them in this life a foretaste of the
consolations which He promises in the next to those ' who
suffer for justice' sake'."

Father Przikwill, another of those missionaries who were
condemned to imprisonment by the Portuguese authorities,

writing to the Father Provincial of Bohemia,* says : " We embarked at Goa in 1761, and were five months at sea. During this painful and sorrowful voyage we lost successively twenty-three of our companions. Their heroism and resignation, their love of God and their confidence, made us look upon their death less as a cause of regret than a matter of envy. At length, on the 20th of May, we arrived at the mouth of the Tagus." They were immediately placed in dungeons thus described: " Our habitation is subterraneous, resembling a deep cavern, or rather the ancient vaults for the interment of the dead. Its proximity to the sea-shore renders it constantly damp. Worms generate and multiply by myriads, from which we suffer much. Vent-holes have been made high up in the walls to afford sufficient light for those who descend to convey us our food ; but neither air nor light can reach us, except only when the iron door of the window is opened. You can judge from this how infectious and unhealthy these subterranean dungeons are. The wretched oil which we burn in our lamp emits an insupportable odour. The cell in which I am is six feet long by thirteen feet wide. On the first day of my arrival I had the damp ground for my bed, and for a pillow my breviary. After some time they gave us a straw bed, which was soon rotted by the damp. Such is the couch upon which I serenely repose. *Blessed be God, the Father of our Lord Jesus Christ, the God of all consolation, who consoles us in all our tribulation,* and who makes us feel how sweet it is to suffer for His holy name. . . . . But what are our sufferings in comparison with those which the Apostle of the Gentiles endured in all His members ? We have, strictly

* Published for the first time by the Rev. Father de Ravignan in *Clement XIII. and Clement XIV.*

speaking, only one source of sorrow, but it is a great one. It is being deprived of the bread of angels. Alas! can you believe it, Reverend Father, they will only grant it to the dying? Oh, how closely do we not resemble the dead! God grant that we may be as perfectly dead to the world. . . . . Thanks be to God, who fortifies me, I desire nothing more than to bear the cross of Jesus Christ, to die with Him, and to do His divine will in all things."

In 1764 eighty additional Jesuits were thrust into the dungeons of St. Julien. One of these prisoners, Father Francis Filipi, formerly missionary of Malabar, tells us: " Not long afterwards, thirty-four of our fellow-prisoners were removed to Rome. Our purgatory was not yet complete; ten long years still remained to be added to our penance. . . . . In 1773, in accordance with the directions of Pombal, we were all collected at the entrance of the dungeons, and, after reading us the decree of the suppression of the Society, they violently tore from our backs the last remnants of the habit of the Society, and in the presence of two companies of soldiers and a large concourse of spectators, who rejoiced in our humiliating position, they clothed us in a parti-coloured sort of hair-cloth garment, resembling a smock-frock, thereby adding to our confusion by its absurd appearance as contrasted with the habit of our Society. Oh, Father, I have not words to expatiate upon these proceedings! Human language is inadequate to express the feelings which rent our hearts. You, too, have participated in the anguish, and are capable of comprehending them. God alone knows the tears, the sighs, and, above all, the extreme consternation of which our catacombs were witness. They jeered at our grief, and reproached us with it as though it were a crime." Although the order was suppressed, these persecuted priests were not released. At last the prison doors were opened in the year 1777, after the inmates had passed sixteen years in a living tomb and thirty-five of their companions had died. During the entire eighteen years of their captivity they had never been interrogated by an agent of the government or informed of the cause of their imprisonment. Hatred and iniquity did not take the trouble of clothing themselves with even a semblance of justice. The deep-seated and intense dislike of the Catholic Church and of the Jesuits which rankled in the bosoms of the freethinkers of Europe found full gratification in the cruel persecutions under the direction of the Marquis de Pombal. To the present day this cruel tyrant is praised by Protestants and infidels as a Liberal statesman. He strangely earned his title to that distinction, and nothing can be more instructive, or more honourable to the Society of Jesus, than the treatment they received and the manner in which it was borne.

It is a most significant fact that those countries which have sowed the wind of infidelism and pseudo-Liberalism have invariably reaped the whirlwind of revolution and civil war. The relaxation of the moral and religious bonds which keep society together has never been effected with impunity. France, Spain, and Portugal permitted the persecution of religion and the banishment of religious orders ; disorganisation, revolution, infidelism, and widespread ruin were the results. Spain and Portugal suffered most heavily. In the latter country, in 1832, one of those special recognitions of truth and justice occurred which are ever memorable. Don Miguel recalled the Jesuits, and the first town which offered itself to the Fathers after their entry into the diocese of Coimbra was that of Pombal, where

the minister of that name lay dead.   There, amidst the
ringing of bells and beautiful illuminations, the Jesuits
entered the church in triumph, and found the body of the
arch-enemy of their order not yet entombed, but lying on
a bier covered with a flag.   One of their first acts was to
celebrate a mass for the repose of the soul of one for whom
it was their duty to pray.   This was the Jesuits' revenge.
At Coimbra, and in other parts of Portugal, the members
of the Society were received with enthusiasm, and the
Countess of Oliveira, niece of the Marquis de Pombal,
declared that it was the duty of her family to repair the
great injustices committed by her uncle.   Greetings of welcome were heard on all sides, but the General (Roothaan)
wisely wrote to Portugal: "To-day Hosanna, humility.
Soon perhaps it will be 'Tolle, crucifige'." The presenti-
ment was fully realised.   Infidelism and immorality were
too strong in Portugal, and the Jesuits were again exiled.

CHAPTER VII

The history of the order in Italy. Progress under various Generals. Bellarmine. St. Aloysius de Gonzaga. Venice. Extraordinary transactions in Malta. Organised infidel attack on the order. The Pope threatened and bullied. Suppression of the order. Survival in Russia. Reinstatement of the order. Infamous calumnies. Recent missions. The distinguished men of the order. Services of the order to mankind.

WE have now to advert to the history of the Society in Italy, the country where the Vicar of Christ and the General of the order are always stationed. The Generalship of St. Ignatius Loyola subsisted from 1541 to 1556, that of Father Laynez from 1554 to 1565, while St. Francis Borgia held the office from 1565 to 1572. During these eventful periods the order grew, under the blessing of God, to be one of the principal bulwarks of His Church. We have seen its Fathers at the Council of Trent, and also combating against both heresy and immorality in the various countries of Europe. Under the rule of Father Laynez a question had arisen as to the General's term of office. By the unanimous written votes of the members it was settled that the General should hold office for life, and this decision was confirmed by the Sovereign Pontiff.

It was on the Feast of the Assumption, in 1583, that the

magnificent Church of the "*Gesu*" in Rome, erected by Cardinal Alexander Farnese at his own expense, was inaugurated by Pope Gregory XIII. This Pope became for ever memorable by the reform of the calendar, entrusted successfully to Father Christopher Clavius, S.J., of Bamberg in Bavaria, who was styled "The Catholic Euclid". Bitter was the opposition to the reception of a truth similar in character to the axiom that two and two make four, because it was enunciated by Jesuits. Voltaire tells us that "the Protestants obstinately persisted in refusing to receive from the Pope a truth, which, had it been proposed by the Turks, they would have willingly accepted". At this period Naples was under Spanish rule, and dearness of provisions formed a pretext for an alarming rebellion, completely quelled by the interference of Father Charles de Mastrelli and other Jesuits whom the people loved. Among the masses the priests of the Society have always been successful whenever really known. Calumnies and unjust misrepresentations are the only barriers to the general appreciation of the enormous value of the Society.

Father Everard Mercurian held the office of General from 1572 to 1580—the time of Elizabeth in England, of Don Juan of Austria, of Peter Canisius in Switzerland, of St. Charles Borromeo in Italy. He was succeeded by Father Claudius Aquaviva (1581 to 1615), who had to exercise great firmness and humility when Pope Sixtus V. desired to change the name of the Society. The numerous alterations which His Holiness desired to effect would have so essentially altered the spirit of the Society that "the Company" of St. Ignatius must have disappeared. The Catholic Sovereigns supported and defended the Society, the General earnestly invoked the help of Almighty God ; but the decree had to be drawn up, and was lying ready for the Pope's signature when a solemn Novena was ordered. The last day of the nine had arrived, and the bell of the Novitiate was calling its members for the litanies, when Sixtus V. expired, leaving the document unsigned which would have virtually destroyed the Society. It was on the 21st of June, 1591, that an angel in human form, the seraphic St. Aloysius Gonzaga, of the Order of Jesus, passed to his reward at the age of twenty-three. The illustrious and learned Father Bellarmine, who had directed and trained this Saint, was forced to accept the Cardinal's hat in 1599. This great man begged, as a favour, that when he died he might be interred at the feet of St. Aloysius Gonzaga.

The Government of the Republic of Venice having put forth decrees in opposition to ecclesiastical rights and immunities, was publicly excommunicated on the 17th of April, 1606. The writings and sermons of Brother Paolo Sarpi and Brother Fulgenzio of the Servite order had, unfortunately, considerably tended to this result. The Jesuits respected the orders of the Vicar of Christ; and, when asked by the Senate what course they intended to adopt, at once replied that so long as the interdict remained in force they would not celebrate mass nor preach, and that if the authorities attempted to compel them they would prefer exile and confiscation. Accordingly, they were driven from Venice; but, in order to blind the public, it was calumniously stated that the reason of their banishment was their being spies of the Pope. It was alleged that the Fathers in Venice had sent to the General of their order detailed accounts of the Venetian forces, finances, &c., and had asked His Holiness to excommunicate the Government. Subsequently, the dreadful events connected with this rebellion against the

Holy See came to an end, and the Jesuits, earnestly desiring the reconciliation of the people of Venice with the Church, implored the Pope to pass over their own claims in order that peace should be made. They thus sacrificed themselves, although greatly against the will of Paul V., who knew well that they had been banished simply for upholding the rights of the Roman Pontiff.

Father Mutius Vitelleschi, the sixth General, ruled the order from 1615 to 1645. During this period the Society was extremely successful in Italy. In Naples Father Pavone founded a congregation of priests which furnished to the Church in a few years one sovereign Pontiff, fifteen bishops, one hundred and eighty prelates, besides a multitude of zealous and devoted priests. No fewer than eighty houses of this Institute were established in various parts of the kingdom. It was in 1617, and in Naples, that Father Peter Ferragut, S.J., established the great *Della Misericordia* confraternity for the help and liberation of prisoners. The Society has frequently distinguished itself by mediating, so as to secure friendship and brotherly love. At Lucca serious misunderstandings between the Bishop and his flock were effectually removed by the intervention of Father Constanzio; and at Malta, when two factions had arisen among the Knights, peace was re-established by means of the exertions of F. Charles Mastrilli. In this island, which St. Paul visited, and whose history is that of chivalry and romance, the brave defenders of the faith found, in enforced want of employment, a Capua in which much laxity and dangerous irregularities prevailed. The Jesuit Fathers in Malta saw that it was their duty to co-operate with the Grand Master (1639) in his efforts to bring back his knights to that Christian life prescribed by the statutes of their order. A theatrical representation, prepared for the Carnival, comprised features of an improper character which could not be tolerated. The Grand Master forbade this play, but stated at the same time that if the Jesuit Father Cassia would say that, in conscience, it could be authorised, the edict would be withdrawn. This priest could not do so, and immediately an outcry arose against the austerity of the Society. Its members were publicly insulted, and the party of revolt, having recourse to arms, ransacked the Jesuit college, and forced the eleven Fathers who resided there to sail for Sicily. So soon as these events became known, Pope Urban VIII. ordered the Jesuits to be reinstated, while Louis XIII. of France sternly demanded reparation for the outrage. The Fathers reoccupied their house amid general feelings of pleasure ; but on the next yearly return of the Carnival there was a renewal of excitement. Again did the Knight Salvatici entreat the Grand Master to permit the forbidden piece to be played. In order to avoid an insurrection the necessary permission was granted; but the people were naturally alarmed, and exclaimed that as the good Fathers had condemned the entertainment, it was possible that God Himself might interfere. At the theatre during the day fixed for the performance, Salvatici quarrelled with the Knight Robert Solaris, who was also one of the actors. The latter, seeing his enemy place his hand on his sword, drew his own with great celerity, and pierced Salvatici to the heart. The play could not be produced, and the verdict of the people was that the tragedy which had been enacted instead conveyed the judgment of God.

Father Vincent Carafa was General from 1645 to 1649, and Fathers Piccolomini and Gottifridi from 1649 to 1652. The tenth General of the order, Father Goswin Nickel, held

office from 1652 to 1661.   The Generals who followed were
Father Paul Oliva (1661-1681); Father Charles de Noyelle
(1681-1687); Father de Santalla (1687-1706); Father Tam-
burini (1706-1730);   Father Francis Retz (1730-1750);
Father Visconti (1750-1755); Father Centurioni (1755-
1757); Father Ricci (1758-1775).   These Generals all did
their work nobly, and governed the order with wisdom, firmness, and justice.   The excellent plan of the holy founder
was fully justified in the strength, stability, and utility of the
Society.   In Italy there was comparative peace, while the
storms of persecution, directed by infidelity, immorality,
heresy, and paganism, fiercely assaulted the order in other
parts of the earth.   In Rome, the heart of the Christian
world, the Generals guided and directed all great works with
that devotion to the Holy See which both increased the
value of the Society's labours and the animosity of its
enemies.

In the second half of the eighteenth century we have seen
the infidel powers of Europe conspiring to destroy the
Society.   Choiseul in France, D'Aranda in Spain, and De
Pombal in Portugal were among the principal leaders of the
infidel party who were at all times aided by Protestantism
in their attacks on the Jesuits.   Infamous calumnies were
followed by barbarous cruelty.   Imprisonment, confiscation,
death, and exile had to be suffered.   Nothing less than the
utter destruction of the Society was intended, and, at last,
it almost seemed as if their enemies had prevailed.   On the
19th of May, 1769, Cardinal Ganganelli was elected Pope
under the title of Clement XIV.   He was a friend of the
Jesuits, and at their recommendation had been appointed a
Cardinal.   On the 16th of June, 1769, D'Alambert, the
freethinking philosopher, wrote to Frederick II., King of

Prussia : " It is said that the Jesuits have little to hope for from the Franciscan Ganganelli, and that St. Ignatius is likely to be sacrificed by St. Francis of Assissium. It appears to me that the Holy Father, Franciscan though he be, would be acting very foolishly thus to disband his regiment of guards simply out of complaisance to Catholic princes. To me it appears that this treaty resembles that of the wolves with the sheep, of which the first condition was that the sheep should give up their dogs; it is well known in what position they afterwards found themselves." Again, on the 7th of August, he writes : " It is asserted that the Franciscan Pope requires to be much importuned regarding the suppression of the Jesuits. I am not at all surprised at it. Proposing to a Pope to abolish that brave militia is like suggesting to your Majesty the disbanding of your favourite guards." All the principal powers of the earth, however, had gathered against this order of Christ. The disciple had to suffer like the Master, and the time of the passion of the Society had come. The Emperor Joseph of Austria, as well as the Prime Ministers of France, Spain, and Portugal, were leagued against the Society. Protestantism dominated Northern Europe and gloated over the spectacle of a general onslaught on the best troops of the Church. Frederick II. of Prussia knew the freethinking philosophers well, and saw clearly that the Jesuits were suffering most unjustly. Writing to D'Alambert, he declares : " The philosophy which is encouraged in our day is more loudly proclaimed than ever. What progress has it made? You will reply, We have expelled the Jesuits. I admit it ; but I can prove to you, if you so desire it, that it was pride, private revenge, cabals, and, in fact, self-interest that accomplished the work." The Pope was conscientiously opposed to the abolition of the

Society of Jesus, and it was consequently necessary to bully and to threaten in order to gain the end in view. The Duc de Choiseul, writing to the French ambassador at Rome, says: "I do not know whether it was well to expel the Jesuits from France and Spain. They have been expelled from all the States of the house of Bourbon. I believe it was even worse when these monks were gone to cause so much excitement in Rome about the suppression of the order, and to allow all Europe to become aware of the attempt. But such is now the case. It so happens that the Kings of France, Spain, and Naples are at open war with the Jesuits and their partisans. Shall they be suppressed, or shall they not? Shall the crowned heads triumph, or are the Jesuits to win the victory? This is the question which now agitates the cabinets, and is the source of all the intrigues, broils, and troubles of all the Catholic courts. In fact we cannot look calmly upon this state of things without being struck by its impropriety; and were I ambassador at Rome, I should feel humiliated to see Father Ricci oppose my royal master." The majority of the sacred college was completely in favour of the Jesuits; and the Pope, finding that they were unshaken in their opinion, became isolated and had to withstand alone a pressure of the most extraordinary and terrible character. His Holiness desired to gain time, and, writing to Louis XV. of France, candidly states: "I can neither censure nor abolish an Institute which has been commended by nineteen of my predecessors. Still less can I do so, since it has been confirmed by the Council of Trent, for according to your French maxims, the General Council is above the Pope. If it be so desired I will call together a general council, in which everything shall be fully and fairly discussed for and against." But the infidel ministers would brook no delay, and in the most importunate manner declared that the King of Spain had become so excited that he would lose his reason unless he obtained a formal promise that the Society would be suppressed. This imbecile Bourbon King was so easily deceived and led that he does not seem to have had much reason to lose ; but it is weak-minded people who become most obstinate and most unreasonable. The French ambassador was threatened with immediate recall if he did not know how to induce the Pope to enter into an official engagement. A letter was extorted from His Holiness to the King of Spain, regarding which Cardinal de Bernis remarks : " This letter which I have caused the Pope to write binds him so irrevocably that, unless the Court of Spain changes its views, the Pope will be compelled in spite of himself to complete the affair ". Threats were used that kingdoms would throw off the allegiance of the Church unless the prayer were granted, and these certainly had some significance when we call to mind the political system of Europe. As Henry VIII. caused the apostasy of England in the 16th century, so was it quite possible for a powerful irresponsible ruler in the 18th century to cause immense injury to religion and to the salvation of souls. It is true that the Protestant or rather infidel King of Prussia was a giant in intellect compared to any of the Bourbon kings, and could not be duped. He knew well that the Jesuits were not only perfectly innocent, but were among the foremost and the best defenders of social order which has revealed religion for its principal support, but he stood almost alone. He knew that the infidels of Europe were merely hastening the revolution by attacking the Jesuits, and therefore declined to join in the persecution of men who were really the firmest

supporters of constituted authority. The astute Empress of
Russia also saw the folly of persecuting staunch friends of
the throne and altar. In her dominions the Jesuits were
specially protected and remained unsuppressed.

In 1772 the Spanish Ambassador determined to terrify the
Pope into submission, and with extraordinary pertinacity
really bullied the Holy See. On one occasion he said in
public audience: " Beware lest my master the king approve
the project which has been entertained by more than one
Court, the suppression of all the religious orders ! If you
would save them do not confound their cause with that of
the Jesuits." "Ah," replied the Pontiff, "I have for a long
time thought that this was what they were aiming at ! They
seek even more—the entire destruction of the Catholic
religion—schism, perhaps heresy. Such are their secret designs." This conversation raises the veil, and shows that the
abolition of the Jesuits was merely considered expedient for
fear of greater evils. The Vicar of Christ was placed in a
dilemma of the most grave and difficult character. He
neither censured the Society nor believed in the absurd
calumnies launched against it, but administering the affairs
of the Church considered it advisable to bow temporarily
to the storm for fear of that greater injury to faith and morals
which might be the sequence of another line of conduct. It
is specially noteworthy that no Bull of suppression was issued,
but merely the brief "Dominus ac Redemptor Noster," which
could be revoked at any-time without difficulty, and was no
way binding on the Pope's successors. The usual formali-
ties for its publication and canonical execution were not
observed, and the bishops were not commanded, but merely
recommended to notify the contents of the brief to those
concerned.

It was on the 21st July, 1773, that the Pope exclaimed in a tone of deep sorrow: "The bells of the Gesu are not ring-ing for the saints; they are tolling for the dead". On the same day His Holiness affixed his signature to the brief sup-pressing the Society. Cardinal Pacca tells us in his Memoirs that after Clement XIV. had affixed his signature "He dashed the document to one side, cast the pen to the other, and from that moment was demented". The awful pressure and the extreme desire to do what was best under circumstances of most fearful difficulty had unhinged the mind of the Pope. He was sane only at intervals, and then deplored with exces-sive grief the misfortune to the Church of which he had been the very unwilling instrument. The Society of Jesus was obedient even unto death, and followed that plan of heroic submission which has always distinguished the order. Father de Ravignan has eloquently said (*Clement XIII. and Clement XIV.*): "The love of the Society, the grace of the Society, the union of the Society, are the results of those hidden gifts which it is difficult to explain or even to comprehend, save by those transformed individuals who constitute this religious family. So when its dissolution is decreed, when vocations are destroyed, the death sentence is pronounced, an unutter-able martyrdom is accomplished. The religious, ceasing to exist as such, and remaining nevertheless attached to his vocation, is a being suddenly disinherited here below of treasures a thousand times more precious to him than country or family—a thousand times more so than his very existence. This sorrow is widely different from that caused by banish-ment or exile." It was on the 16th of August, 1773, that a Prelate, accompanied by soldiers and agents of the police, notified at the Gesu that the Society was suppressed through-out the world, and on the 22nd of September following Father

Ricci, the General; Father Canelli, Secretary-General; Fathers Le Forestier, Zaccharia, Gauthier, and Faure were confined in the Castle of Saint Angelo.   Wild and outrageous charges were brought against the Society, and it was greatly for its honour and its interest that it should be formally tried.   If any real guilt existed there can be no doubt that it would have been discovered and exposed.   The archives of the Society from the time of St. Ignatius were at the disposal of the prosecution, and all the papers and documents of the Society, even of the most private character, had been seized. All the prisoners were examined and every possible investigation made with the result that there were no treasures, no conspiracies, no guilt.   Father Ricci, the General, who died in prison in November, 1775, at the age of seventy-two, received the last sacrament just previous to his dissolution, and then in a loud and clear voice most solemnly declared in the presence of God that the Society of Jesus had given no cause for suppression, and that he had given no cause for his own imprisonment.   At the same time he did not pretend to attach any guilt to those who injured the Society, and forgave them most earnestly and from his heart.   The Pope himself had died previously—on the 22nd of September, 1774.   He had perfectly recovered his faculties, and his death was a holy one.*   In reality two martyrs suffered from the persecution of infidelism : one was the General of the Society, and the other was the Pope.   It is absolutely clear that the latter was an upright man who was really terri-

---

* It is narrated that on the 21st September, 1774, St. Alphonsus de Liguori fell into a trance which lasted a day and night, upon awaking from which he informed his attendants that he had gone to assist the Pope, who was no more.   At the exact moment in which St. Alphonsus had awakened it was discovered that Pope Clement XIV. had passed into eternity.

fied into proceeding against an order which he loved and respected simply because he feared that if this were not done nations might be alienated from the faith and service of God. What was possible towards the close of the eighteenth century fortunately cannot now be repeated. The spread of education and of liberty are among the greatest bulwarks of the Church. The Bourbon constitutions have for ever passed away, and Kings can no longer dispose of the consciences of their people in the style of Henry VIII. The Monarchs who opposed a Society which was one of the pillars of order displaced solid supports of their own government and hastened a revolution which their own corruption and crimes had so long invited. Frederick of Prussia possessed a mind of superior calibre, and did not care to play into the hands of the *sans culottes*. Writing from Potsdam to his agent in Rome on the 13th September, 1773, he says that in the treaty of Breslau he had guaranteed the *status quo* of the Catholic religion, and he had never found better priests in every respect than the Jesuits. " I am resolved to retain them in my States." The Empress of Russia did not merely approve of the Society, but gave the strictest orders that they were to remain in her dominions.

That great Protestant thinker Leopold Ranke, in his history of the Papacy, tells us, that the overthrow of the Jesuits was chiefly attributable to their defence of the supremacy of the See of Rome ; and that as they had made the instruction of youth a special business, their overthrow convulsed the Catholic world to its very centre, and inspirited immensely the enemies of the Church. Those enemies had taken the outworks, and at once proceeded, with great ardour, to the attack of the fortress. The agitation increased from day to day, while desertion and apostasy

thinned the ranks of Catholicism.* The commission at
Rome, charged with the trial of the Jesuits, finished their
labours under the pontificate of Pius VI., the successor of
Clement XIV. They did not find the slightest ground of
accusation against the Society ; the prisoners were set free ;
the Order of Jesus was declared innocent ; and thus was
exhibited the spectacle of a religious order free from blame,
made the Quintus Curtius of the Church, and hurled into
the dangerous social gulf caused by infidelity.

Pope Pius VI. in 1776 issued a decree, virtually em-
powering the Jesuits to establish novitiates in Russia, and
in 1782, a Vicar-General of the order was appointed in that
country. There the Society was still providentially maintained. In Prussia the Jesuits were retained, but they were
not allowed to establish novitiates. In other parts of the
world they were a scattered flock, but still labouring for the
greater glory of God, and distinguished as men of science
and skilful educators of youth. Father Walcher planned the
great dikes of Lake Rofner-lise, and became chief of naviga-
tion and mathematical sciences under the government of
the Empress Maria Theresa. Father Cabral preserved the
city of Terni from the floods of the river Velino, and
subsequently saved a portion of Portugal by constructing
dikes on the banks of the Tagus. Father Riccati regulated
the course of the rivers Po, Adige, and Brenta. Father
Ximenes invented a new and improved system of bridges for
Tuscany and Rome. Father Zeplichal successfully directed
mining operations at Glatz for King Frederick of Prussia. In
France the pulpits were occupied by ex-Jesuits; in Italy many
of the best and most successful seminaries were managed
by Fathers of the order under direction and approval of

---

* Ranke's *History of the Papacy*, Book viii., p. 240.

the Bishops. Throughout the civilised world members of
the suppressed order achieved triumph, and in the midst of
these events one of their greatest enemies, when about to be
summoned before the judgment seat of God, declared that
he had been guilty of the vilest deceit in order to poison the
mind of the King of Spain against the Society. The Duke
of Alba in his last moments stated that he had forged the
fatal letter from the General of the order, which was one of
the principal causes of their destruction. In Portugal De
Pombal was convicted of crimes, condemned to death and
banished. He had restored the confiscated property of his
victims, and retired hated and execrated by the people.
According to his own admission he had expended eight
hundred thousand ducats in effecting the ruin of the
Society. It was only on the accession of Donna Maria to
the throne of Portugal that more than six hundred Fathers
of the Society who had languished in dungeons were released.
They earnestly demanded a trial, as they had been the victims
of malicious falsehood. In the entire history of the world
no more unjustifiable acts of tyranny can be shown than those
perpetrated by De Pombal upon the Order of Jesus, yet this
statesman is persistently praised for deeds which would have
been considered barbarous if directed against any other class
of men than that banded together for the greater glory of
God under the banner of Ignatius Loyola.

In Parma the influence of the Marquis de Felina, the
deadly enemy of the order, having been removed by death,
the colleges were restored to the Jesuits, and the direction
of the University confided to them. This fact is very significant. In truth, the Jesuits were not persecuted by the
people, unless, as in Protestant countries, the minds of the
multitude had been systematically poisoned by calumnies.

The freethinkers of Europe, who hastened the revolution, had really seized upon the reins of Government in France, Spain, Portugal, Naples, and Parma; and it is to them, and to their machinations and hatred, that we owe the temporary subversion of an order which was one of the principal bulwarks both of Christianity and of order. Divine providence had interposed in Russia for the preservation of the order; and on the 7th of March, 1801, in response to a special request from the Emperor Paul, the Bull, *Catholicæ Fidei*, re-established the Society in his dominions. Almost at the same time Charles VII. authorised the return of the Jesuits to Spain, although shortly afterwards they were again proscribed in that kingdom.

At Polotsk on the 4th of October, 1802, Father Gruber was elected General of the Society. Shortly previous to this time—in the year 1800—Thomas Weld had presented the estate of Stonyhurst, in the North of England, to the order, and now an authorisation was issued by the Holy See incorporating this House with the Society in Russia. On the 22nd of May, 1803, Father Marmaduke Stone was appointed Provincial of England. Almost simultaneously a North American Mission under Father Molyneux was organised. In August, 1804, King Ferdinand of Naples reinstated the Jesuits in his dominions, but subsequent disasters forced them to leave. The fiery and comet-like career of Napoleon disorganised Europe, and caused great sufferings to the Church in its head and members. Pius the Seventh became a prisoner, and the Society suffered with the afflicted Church of God. Napoleon had scoffed at his excommunication, and mockingly asked if the Pope imagined that the weapons would fall from the hands of his soldiers.* The Almighty

* See Alison's *History of Europe* for conclusive evidence on this subject.

answered by the events of the retreat from Russia, when the
elements conquered the conqueror, and the lance, sword, and
musket dropped from the nerveless grasp of the French soldier. The Jesuits devoted themselves to the necessities of that
brave and unfortunate army. They nursed the sick, tended
the wounded, and died doing their duty. Father Thaddeus
Brzozowski had become the twentieth General of the order,
and it was to the Russian dominions that its principal efforts
were directed. But the fall of Napoleon meant the firm
reinstatement of the temporal power of the Pope, and the
restoration of the Jesuits to the entire Catholic world.
Heresy and infidelity had their time of triumph, but it was
now passed, and on the 7th of August, 1814, in the Church
of the Gesu in Rome, in presence of the Sovereign Pontiff,
and of eighty-six Fathers * of the order, the Bull fully re-
establishing the Society of Jesus was publicly read.

In Spain, throughout Italy, in Switzerland, Holland,
Belgium, even in South America, the Society was quickly
re-established. Charles Emmanuel, King of Sardinia and
Piedmont, entered its ranks. A powerful reaction set in,
and the world, which had persecuted, now favoured and protected. As instructors of youth the Jesuits were specially
needed, and this has been and is the principal work to which,
in Europe, they have devoted their efforts. A true Christian
education is the bulwark of order, and in erecting this sound
fortification the members of the Society continue to be indefatigable and successful. The Prince de Talleyrand, one of
the most acute and able statesmen of modern times, addressing
Louis XVIII., told him emphatically that if he were desirous of remaining at the Tuileries he should take the neces-

* One of these Fathers, Albert de Montaldo, was 126 years of age, and
had entered the Society on the 12th of September, 1706.

sary precautions, and that the re-establishment of the Society
of Jesus was the surest means of providing that good solid
education which can alone secure peace to future genera-
tions.   In France the Fathers had a difficult and dangerous
task to perform, but established themselves in many parts
of the kingdom ; although at Brest they were expelled by
insurgent bands, who paraded the streets shouting "Death to
the Jesuits !" "Down with Christ and religion !" In North
America the order became widespread and successful.   In
1819 there were no fewer than eighty-six members in the
Missions of Maryland.   In Russia, on the other hand, a
time was come when it seemed as if that country had
accomplished its mission.   The young Prince Galetzin, son
of the Minister of Public Instruction, proclaimed himself a
Catholic, and several other nobles were suspected of joining
the Church. · The Jesuits were immediately persecuted, and
when the Father-General naturally desired to leave for
Rome permission was refused.   The twentieth General was
forced to die in Russia, foretelling that his spiritual children
would shortly be expelled from the empire.   They were
driven forth by an imperial decree dated 13th March, 1820.
On the 18th October of the same year, Father Louis Fortis
was elected the twenty-first General, and the headquarters
of the order was re-established in Rome.

Austria opened its arms to the Jesuits who had been
banished from Russia.   In 1822 the field of the operations
of the Society included Ireland, while in England, where its
members had been formerly fiercely persecuted, they now
established a Home, which, in these latter days, has become
a Refuge.   Over Spain, on the other hand, which had formerly been glorious in its achievements for the faith, the
wretched spirit of infidelity had obtained considerable power,

and the Jesuits were persecuted with such implacable ferocity that twenty-three Fathers, who were in course of being conducted to Barcelona as prisoners, were massacred. This foul deed was committed on the 17th of November, 1822, in the name of "liberty and fraternity". The colonies of this formerly great nation had been deprived of the Jesuits by arbitrary orders from the mother country. Civilisation, education, and order were owing to the efforts of the Society, and when the workmen were withdrawn the work stopped, revolution and immorality stepped in, Spain lost its possessions, and petty republics, torn with intestine quarrels, took its place.

Pius VII. died in 1823, and was succeeded by Leo XII., who granted to the Society the Roman College, the Church of St. Ignatius and the oratory, as well as the museums, library, and observatory. In Austria the order was extremely useful, and received the steady support of the Emperor. In Holland, on the other hand, the King was opposed to the Jesuits, and did everything in his power to thwart them. At this time a celebrated paper of the time, named *The Constitutional*, published the most astounding romances, which were, nevertheless, believed by immense numbers, and tended very seriously to prejudice the public mind. The writers in this wide-spread anti-Catholic organ rivalled the authors of *The Arabian Nights* in powers of imagination. The Jesuit establishment at Montrouge was described as an arsenal and fortress, where immense vaults, passing under the bed of the Seine, led to the palace of the Tuileries. Vast treasures were concealed there, and in gloomy recesses secret councils were held, in which bishops were designated, and the *de facto* government of France was carried on. This silly nonsense

was used as a means of frightening the multitude of thought-
less people, always glad to hear and to believe calumnies.
The success of these literary escapades emboldened a writer
named Arnaud to publish an infamous book, styled the
Modern Jesuits, an idea of which can be formed from the
fact that he describes Father Gury as a ferocious tyrant.
He says: "At the very sight of the tyrant of Montrouge
every one trembles. . . . . Read the history of the old man
of the mountain and, perhaps, you will have to acknowledge,
after all, that the old man of the mountain possessed some
feeling. . . . . His novices would unhesitatingly attempt to
lay the world in ashes, if so they might hope to gain the
merit of entire obedience."   In France the ignorant and
insensate hatred of the Jesuits was so fed by preposterous
calumnies that Charles X. weakly succumbed to a demand
for injustice; and, against the advice of the Bishops, deprived
the youth of France of the sound Christian instruction im-
parted by the Society.   The Liberals virtually said : "Sacrifice the Jesuits and Sodalists, and we will support you in the
Chamber".   "Down with the Jesuits," was a much more
common cry than "Down with the throne," but really
meant the same thing.   Promises by revolutionists are
generally only made to be broken, and there was no exception in this case.   On the 29th of July, 1830, King Charles
X., with all his family, had to fly from the kingdom.   A
maniacal hatred of the Society possessed the Liberals, show-
ing itself in attacks on the property and persons of the
Fathers, and in such displays as that at the College of St.
Acheul, when a band of ruffians shouted : " Hurrah for the
Chamber ! hurrah for hell ! down with everything ".

On the 9th of July, 1829, Father John Roothaan became
the twenty-second General.   It would be tiresome to detail

all the persecutions of the party of revolution and of infidelity. A time has come when, in consequence of the
advance of education, it is no longer possible to spread
absurd calumnies with former facility and impunity; nevertheless, illogical prejudices, based upon preconceived notions,
continually militate against the Society. In Protestant
countries latent bigotry is easily aroused, and to the Jesuits
still gloriously applies the words used by our Saviour:
"They have hated me without a cause". The great work
of Father Ravignan, *De l'existence et de l'Institute des
Jesuites*, completely, thoroughly, and triumphantly refutes
the calumnies by means of which the Society was defamed.
The eminent anti-Christian Liberal, Roger Collard, writing
of this work, states that it fully convinces him " of the energy
of that extraordinary Society. . . . . We may say that
Lycurgus and Sparta, although as far removed as earth is
from heaven, were the cradle of St. Ignatius. Sparta has
passed away; the Jesuits will never pass away. They possess a principal of immortality in Christianity, and in the
warlike passions of men." But nothing daunts the enemies
of Christianity. The Jesuits demonstrated the innocence of
their order, but that did not stop a constant flow of calumny
prompted by hatred. *The Wandering Jew*, by an im-
moral writer named Eugene Sue, published in the columns
of the *Constitutionel*, was an atrocious libel on the Society
in the form of a romance, as truthful and reliable as the tales
of *Jack the Giant Killer* and *Cinderella*. Another
writer, already referred to, who had most vigorously assailed
the Jesuits, found it desirable before his death to tell the
truth. On the 27th of August, 1845, Martial Marcet de la
Roche Arnaud " solemnly declared, and in good faith,"
that "I entirely disapprove and contradict all the writings I

have ever published against the Jesuits in 1827, 1828, and 1829—not that I deny having issued them, but I condemn them as the shameful fruits of a vengeance full of deceit; and as such I now submit them, as I have long since done, to the censure of all, or, if it may be, to eternal oblivion. . . . I declare most emphatically that I wantonly, falsely, and without provocation heaped outrageous slanders upon the Jesuits by base personal abuse."

The want of any evidence against the order to justify the hatred and abuse of which it is the object was strikingly exemplified when Rossi arrived at Rome as Ambassador from France to demand the secularisation of the French Jesuits. The Pope called for proofs, but none were forthcoming. The Apostles of "Liberty" wished a body of men to be condemned unheard and without any adequate evidence. His Holiness was told of the unpopularity of the Society, and of the noise and clamour continually poured out against it, but very properly looked upon these facts as so many eulogiums, knowing that Christians flocked in crowds to hear Jesuit sermons, and besieged their confessionals. Louis Phillippe was disappointed, and, to save the credit of his Government, at last asked the Society itself to make some compromise; which, for the sake of peace and conciliation, was effected by a temporary dispersion of some of the Fathers in the principal cities. Immediately, with the mendacity which so unfortunately distinguishes the anti-Catholic press, the *Moniteur* announced that the negotiation with which M. Rossi was charged had been entirely successful, and "that the congregation of Jesuits will cease to exist in France". The Cardinal Secretary of State subsequently declared that His Holiness was greatly surprised, as he had made no concession, and that if any action had been taken it would have been strictly in conformity with the sacred canons. This incident is significant, as it is a specimen of the manner in which falsehood has been persistently used against the Holy See and the Jesuits. The leading Liberal papers in Europe constantly manufactured news inimical to religion, while correspondents from Rome cut their coat according to their cloth, and served up pabulum suitable to the palates of the readers of such papers as the *Constitutionel* and the *London Times*. As it has been justly said that, previous to the time of Dr. Lingard, there was in England a conspiracy against truth so far as history is concerned, so it can be truly stated that for many years, and even in some quarters at the present day, a journalistic conspiracy can be traced against the truth of contemporary history in matters affecting the Holy See and the Catholic Church.

The Society had been partially reinstated in Portugal, but in 1834—so soon as Don Pedro had conquered the country—they were harshly driven out. In Spain the Jesuits were accused of poisoning the public fountains. The agents of the revolution declared that they had found papers of arsenic, which children declared had been given them by the Fathers to scatter about. Anything more preposterous than this charge it is difficult to imagine, and as the men accused were never put on their trial nor allowed any opportunity of defence, the persecution which followed was as completely unjustifiable as it is possible to conceive. The National Guards and the mob, incited by infidel and reactionary leaders, broke into the Imperial College at Madrid, shouting, "Death to priests and monks! Hurrah for liberty!" Eight Fathers were quickly murdered; and, as the blood of these martyrs had not yet satiated the rage of their enemies, Father Jose Fernandez was dragged through the streets amidst blows and insults.   Father Sauri was stabbed to death, and four other Fathers were shot down at the door of the College, and their naked bodies contumeliously exposed to the mob.   Pillage and destruction followed.   At the end of this awful explosion of infidel and revolutionary rage it was found that the assassinated religious comprised fifteen Jesuits, seven Dominicans, forty-four Franciscans, and eight Fathers of Mercy.   On the 17th of July, 1835, the Society of Jesus was abolished throughout Spain by royal decree.

In the United States of America, as well as in Belgium, Holland, England, and Austria, the Society flourished.   No country is so suitable for the order as a free one, where education is widely spread, and where its members can be heard without fear, favour, or prejudice.   Whenever the dreadful cholera epidemic breaks forth, the Fathers now, as formerly, are distinguished by their devotion ; and when in Gallicia they were providentially spared, it was remarked by Father Passerot of the Redemptorists that " it was proper the exterminating angel should respect the name of the Lamb, which you bear as much as of old He did the blood which was His type ".   In Switzerland the order was so thoroughly identified with the vanguard of the Church that one of the radical journals declared, in 1845 : " No doubt the Jesuits are our worst enemies ; but our victory would not be complete even though we succeeded in destroying the last of the sons of Loyola.   There is another power that desires our ruin, and would wish to bind us in chains.   That power is the Papacy."   In Italy the order was favoured by Charles Albert, King of Piedmont, who, in answer to the opposition of the University of Genoa, declared that as he could not find a house in that city for the Jesuits he would give them his own. In Rome Gregory XVI. solemnly placed the great College of the Propaganda under the direction of the Society. As regards foreign missions, volumes could be written on the labours of the Fathers of the order. Practically, they may be said to have acquired for Christianity that vast territory which lies between the United States and the Pacific Ocean north of California, formed into three dioceses, under the administration of one Archbishop and two suffragan Bishops. The Jesuits were special missionaries to the natives of the two Americas. On the Rocky Mountains, as on the Orinoco and on the Amazon, they converted nations to Christianity. Nothing could surpass the devotion, fervour, and zeal of the missioners except their success. Father de Sinet, who has been aptly termed the Apostle of the Rocky Mountains, travelled five thousand miles within eight months, saw five of his companions perish in the rapids of the Columbia River, crossed the various chains of the Rocky Mountains, traversed the desert of the Yellowstone in its greatest width, and descended the Missouri to St. Louis. The Society had everywhere to fight against the inclemency of nature in some countries, against the savagery of man in others. Neither arctic cold nor tropic heat were, however, such dangerous enemies as the passions of men. In the Argentine Republic the civilisers, protectors, and pastors of South America were called upon to support the cruel despotism of Rosas, and preferred to do their duty and to be driven into exile. In Syria and in the Levant the persecutions of Turkish fanaticism * had to be endured ; while at Goa, in India, they had to encounter the narrow hatred of the miscalled

* In the single town of Saida alone twenty Jesuits were found among the killed.

Portuguese liberals. The British power, however, was favourable to the Society throughout its immense empire in the East. Hindostan has become, under God, one of the most extensive and most successful missionary fields of the Society. On the 27th of April, 1841, Fathers Gotteland, Brueyre, and Esteve embarked at Brest for China, and found on their arrival in the province of Canton no fewer than forty-five thousand Christians, who had preserved the faith since the suppression of the order. Hundreds of intrepid Fathers have followed ; and in this great field of immense difficulty and danger, as well as of immense fruit, a great Christian empire will yet be raised on the ruins of Bhuddism. In the prisons of Toulon, and among the convents of Cayenne, the Jesuits laboured most assiduously, and with a great blessing, while in Algeria a new field is ably and successfully worked.

At the present day the tree planted by Ignatius, and fertilised by the sufferings and martyrdoms of so many of his sons, is greater and more flourishing than at any previous time. Its branches stretch over the world, and under its shade the Gospel is preached in the four quarters of the world. Their sound has gone forth throughout all the earth, and their words to the end of the world. There are missions in China, Canada, the United States of North America, Guiana, Algiers, South Africa, Central Africa, Syria, New Orleans, Madura, Bourbon, Madagascar, Fernando Po ; at the Antilles, in Guatemala, Honduras, Chili, Brazil, and La Plata ; in Bombay, Calcutta, California, and Oregon ; in Australia and Java ; in Dalmatia, Illyria, Albania, Sicily, Holland, and England.

If the tree be judged by its fruits, the Order of Jesus stands forth as one of the most glorious and noble institutions which has helped to support, to defend, and to teach Christianity. The Society has given to the world and to Heaven St. Ignatius Loyola its founder, St. Francis Xavier the Apostle of the Indies, St. Francis Borgia, St. John Francis Regis, St. Francis de Hieronimo, Apostle of Naples, St. Aloysius Gonzaga, and St. Stanislaus Kostka; the three canonised martyrs of Japan—Paul Miki, John de Gotto, and James Kisai; the Blessed Alphonsus Rodriguez, Peter Claver, Andrew Bobola, John de Britto, Peter Canisius, Father Ignatius Azavedo, and his thirty-nine companions; the Venerable Rudolph Aquaviva and his four companions, Joseph Anchieta, Bernardin Realin, Louis du Pont, and John Berchmans. Many other names of men of extraordinary sanctity could be mentioned in a chain stretching from the present day to the origin of the Society. The education of youth was one of the greatest and most successful works. Lord Bacon * emphatically tells us that it is impossible to improve upon their mode of instruction, and Leibnitz † agrees with him. Their editions of the classics and works of instruction were so good that ‡ Macaulay aptly and correctly says that the name of a Jesuit on the title page of a book ensured its success. Long lists of great teachers and great writers could be given.§ They became distinguished in natural philosophy, chemistry, botany, mathematics, mechanics, astronomy, poetry, history, languages, antiquities. There was no branch of science which was not cultivated by Jesuits with distinguished success. Illustrious pontiffs, princes, generals, magistrates, men of learning, authors who

---

* *De Dignitate et Aug. Scientiæ.*, lib. vii., p. 153.
† *Works of Leibnitz*, tome vi., p. 65.
‡ Article in Edinburgh Review.
§ See Cretineau Joly's *Histoire*, vol. iv.

will be the eternal glory of their respective countries, were
formed mentally within their schools. The aid given to the
study of theology and of sacred history by Fathers of the
order has been of an extraordinarily valuable character. To
prove this it is only necessary to cite the works of such men
as Suarez, Nasquez, Molina, Cornelius a Lapide, Bellarmine,
Tolet, Sirmond, Theophile, Labbe, Alvarez, Arias, Denis
Petau, Rodriguez. The best annotated edition of *The
Imitation of Jesus Christ* was by F. Jerome Gonnelieu, while
F. Jean Brignon popularised in France *The Spiritual Com-
bat.* *Christian Perfection* was from the pen of F. Rodriguez,
Pia Desideria by F. de Boissieu, *Doctrine Spirituelle* by F.
Lallemant, the Catechism and the Dialogues of F. Joseph
Surin were recommended by Bossuet, *The Devotion to the
Sacred Heart of Jesus* was written by F. de Gallifet. Religion
was explained and popularised, devotion spread and count-
less souls saved. In philosophy, metaphysics, and history
the Society produced such writers as Fabri, Garnier, Cossart,
Brunet, Lorin, Giattini Stengel, Pallavicini, Hauser, du
Phanjas, Suarez, Pereira, Rapin. The Company has always
been celebrated for its eloquent preachers. No period has
been without them, and a mere list would far exceed the
limits of this work. Such historians as Pallavicini (*History
of the Council of Trent*), Mariana (*History of Spain, The
Wars of the Low Countries*), Turselin (*Universal History*),
Daniel (*History of France*), D'Avrigny (*Chronological
Memoirs*), Longueval (*History of the Church in France*), De
Charlevoix (*History of Japan, &c., &c.*), Besson (*Syria
Sacra*), Du Halde (*History, Geography, &c., of China, Lettres
Edifiantes, &c.*), Berruyer (*History of the People of God*).
Rosweyde, Jean Bolland, and other Fathers conceived and
carried on the great design of the lives of the Saints, afterwards

so nobly and so successfully completed by the Benedictines. The Laws of the Church, as well as general jurisprudence, were treated of with the utmost ability by such writers as Lineck, Schwartz, Stefanucci, Biner. The canonists of the Company were as celebrated as its historians and lexicographers. In mathematics the order became *facile princeps*, and such names can be cited as Clavius, Gregoire de Saint Vincent, de la Faille, Guldin, Lalouere, Nicolas, Kresa le Morave, Ceva, Vincent Riccati. The algebraic labours and treatise on the integral calculus of the last named have never been surpassed. Riccioli and Grimaldi confirmed the teachings of Galileo. It was Grimaldi who added five hundred and five stars to the catalogue of Kepler, and whose treatise on the light and colours of the iris supplied Sir Isaac Newton with the fundamental principles on which he based his work on optics. Father Paul L'Hoste became celebrated for his *Treatise on the Construction of Vessels and on Naval Tactics*, while Father Charles Borgo admirably explained *The Art of Fortification and of the Defence of Places.* Zucchi Kircher, Schott, Cesi, and a host of others were among the most celebrated mathematicians, scientific dicoverers, and natural philosophers of their time. As geographical discoverers, the Jesuits have always held a high place. The four quarters of the world have been travelled over and described by Fathers of the order. Early in the seventeenth century Father Peter Paez published his *Relation of the Discovery of the Sources of the Nile.* In 1740 F. Manuel Ramon arrived at the point of junction of the Orinoco and Maragnon rivers in South America. The first white man who traversed Lake Michigan and traced the Mississippi to the Gulf of Mexico was a Jesuit Priest. Oregon owes its discovery to the Society, and it was F.

Abanel who opened up a safe land route to Hudson's Bay.
In 1614 F. Biard fully described the eastern portion of
Canada; in 1620 F. Jerome des Angelis was the first
European who penetrated into the country of Yesso; in
1626 F. Charles Lallemant made the world acquainted with
the regions near Quebec. About the same period F.
Antony de Andrada advanced to the hitherto unknown
sources of the Ganges. The same Jesuit travelled through
great Thibet, whose existence had been hitherto almost
unknown in Europe. In 1674 FF. Bechamel and Grillet
explored the deserts of Guiana, and on the same continent
F. Fritz ascended the Amazon to its source. In Japan,
China, India, North and South America, and Africa they
gained treasures of geographical knowledge. Among other
material advantages secured by them for mankind we may
mention various valuable medicines, such as rhubarb and
quinine, discovered and introduced into Europe. From the
forests of South America they brought for general use indian
rubber and vanilla, as well as the bark of the Chinchona
tree. They became the means of introducing special
improvements from India into the art of dyeing clothes, and
transferred from China to Europe the art of porcelain manu-
facture. These facts are stated merely as illustrations. It
would require volumes to narrate the services of the Society
to geographical discovery, to the arts and sciences, and to the
general advancement of piety and of learning. Above all
things the Jesuits are missionaries. The four quarters of
the world bear witness to their sufferings and labours. The
vocal blood of their martyrs cries aloud in testimony of the
labours, sufferings, and success of the order in Japan, China,
India, North America, South America, and Europe. They
have died for Jesus Christ on the scaffolds of England, under

the guillotines of France, on the crosses of Japan, under the tortures of savages, and as victims of revolutionary fury. They have constantly been the victims of calumny, insult, and spoliation. In truth, they have nobly earned the title they bear. The servant is not greater than his master. The Company of Jesus must expect to be treated like their Lord; and the prayer of St. Ignatius Loyola that his Society might always suffer persecution has been heard. A rough, imperfect, and very brief sketch has now been furnished of the history of this great order. It will serve its purpose if it but call attention to a subject of great importance, dispel some prejudices, and lead readers to the study of larger and more complete histories of the Society of Jesus.

THE END.

Now in preparation, price ONE SHILLI...

THE

THIRD EDITION—CAREFULLY REVISED

OF THE

STORY

OF THE

SCOTTISH REFORMATION

By A. WILMOT,

AUTHOR OF "THE HISTORY OF THE JESUITS,"

Accompanied by a Letter from the Hon. COLIN LIN...

———⁕⬦⁕———

THIS Work has been most favour...
received by the Catholic Press, and ...
the only one issued in popular for.n
which contains the true history of the so-called
Reformation in Scotland. All the facts
lating to the Presbyterian Apostle, John Kn...
are fully disclosed.